Overtime
Tactical Protectors
M.D. Dalrymple

Book 3

Copyright 2019 Michelle Deerwester-Dalrymple
ISBN: 9798326583796

Imprint: Independently published

Sword and Thistle LLC

Images licensed through Canva.com

All rights reserved. In accordance with the U.S. Copyright Act of 1976, the scanning, uploading, distribution, or electronic sharing of any part of this book without the permission of the author constitutes unlawful piracy of the author's intellectual property. If you would like to use the material from this book, other than for review purposes, prior authorization from the author must be obtained. Copies of this text can be made for personal use only. No mass distribution of copies of this text is permitted.

This book is a work of fiction. Names, dates, places, and events are products of the author's imagination or used factiously. Any similarity or resemblance to any person living or dead, place, or event is purely coincidental.

Bonus Police Ebook

Don't forget to grab your **bonus ebook** police romance ebook starter! Click the image below to receive *On Patrol*, a pulled-from-real-life short story in your inbox, plus more freebies, ebooks, and goodies!

Then, check out my other *Tactical Protectors* series, my police series, and ride along with the boys in blue! Look for all the books in the *Tactical Protectors* series today!

Click here: https://swordandthistle.myflodesk.com/bee17851-69cc-4148-a553-c97b2134f60b

Contents

1. One — 1
2. Two — 7
3. Three — 13
4. Four — 21
5. Five — 28
6. Six — 32
7. Seven — 39
8. Eight — 44
9. Nine — 52
10. Ten — 62
11. Eleven — 69
12. Twelve — 74

Bonus Police Ebook — 81

Police Blotter — 83

Excerpt from Charming: — 85

About the Author — 91

Also By Michelle — 93

ONE

Tyrell wiped the sweat from his brow. His beat partner, Matthew, had really taken the idea of working out to a new level. When he asked Tyrell if he could join him at the gym a couple times a week, how could Tyrell say no?

It wasn't like he didn't go to the gym. Hell, his slick, muscled, physique, coupled with his commanding height and perfect ebony skin made him a coveted prize at his fitness center, and he kept all that going by hitting the gym no less than five times a week. Phone numbers on slips of paper or women "accidentally" bumping into him were regular occurrences. He was on a first name basis with all the trainers and instructors, had a regular reservation for the basketball court on Saturday mornings and the racquetball court on Tuesdays. The rest of the time, it was all heavy weights, baby.

Of course, Tyrell invited Matthew on Wednesdays and Fridays for lifting. Those were his easier days, and he didn't want to kill his own beat partner with the heavy lifting. At least, not yet. Tyrell smiled at the thought, his brilliant white teeth a stark and handsome contrast to his full lips, and another young woman, this one on the treadmill walking her way to nowhere, winked at him.

Matthew did not miss the interaction.

"Jeez, Blaser, is there anywhere you go where women don't throw themselves at you?"

Tyrell turned that gleaming grin to Matthew as he grabbed the heavy barbell Matthew just dropped with one hand.

"Show-off," Matthew commented as Tyrell added more weights.

"You'll get there, Danes," Tyrell promised, his voice rolling like ocean waves.

Adding two 45-pound plates to each side, Tyrell began his own set of dead lifts, pulling the barbell off the ground to his waist three times. He paused, then prepped for another set of three. The lifting was getting easier; he would have to add more weight in the next week or two, he thought before grabbing the bar again.

Matthew said something to him as Tyrell dropped the bar for the final time, and he missed his partner's comment.

"What'd you say?"

"Rosemarie wants you over for dinner, maybe this week?"

Tyrell noted the sheepish smile on Matthew's blonde face, and Tyrell gave him another smile. But this time it was more of a smirk.

"Ugh, Danes," Tyrell exhaled, wiping sweat off his forehead with a blue and white gym towel, "she is not trying to set me up again, is she?"

Matthew dipped his head low, not wanting to look his partner in the eyes. He knew she was, but Tyrell would never show up if he admitted the full truth. Unfortunately, Matthew's open face hid little. He decided to hedge just a bit.

"Not really. And would it work if she did? She knows you are not ready to settle down at all, but she thinks you are way too good looking to be single." Matthew took a swig of his water bottle and then grinned stupidly at his friend. "If she wasn't so into me, I would almost be worried at how she talks about you, brother."

Matthew clapped Tyrell on the shoulder, and Tyrell nearly laughed out loud at the comment. His beat partner teased him mercilessly over his "manscaping," as he called it. To hear him talk about how much his own girlfriend liked it struck Tyrell as funny. Tyrell punched Matthew's arm in return.

"Ok, I'll go, set up or not. If nothing else, to get some of Rosemarie's great cooking. Now, quit talking and start lifting. We have another set to do before we switch up for the overhead."

After giving Tyrell a mocking salute, Matthew removed the extra plates before attempting another lift.

They had Tuesday night off, so that made selecting a night easy. Rosemarie was known for her funky concoctions that seemed to work, and tonight was no different. When Tyrell arrived, a subtle aroma of meat and cheese hung in the air, with a stronger scent of garlic as a chaser. She called the light meal a "charcuterie platter" — a popular dish at her wine bar.

"A charcuterie platter? Fancy," Tyrell complimented as he kissed Rosemarie on the cheek.

Her own fruity-scented hair briefly displaced the aroma from dinner, and for a moment, Tyrell envied his beat partner and the woman he came home to every night. Playing the field was fun, and Tyrell was only twenty-seven and uncertain he was ready to settle down, as Rosemarie had said — but when he was around Matthew and Rosemarie, he thought differently.

She passed him a gracious smile as wisps of her blue-black hair framed her face. Leading him to the kitchen, she gestured at the platter.

"Yes, help yourself. There's also fruit, honey, and crackers. We are having a garlic pesto pasta for dinner. Sound good?"

Tyrell nodded, his mouth full of meat and cheese, and searched the kitchen and living area with nervous eyes. If Rosemarie invited a blind date to meet him, Tyrell saw no evidence of her. Matthew's voice boomed from the hall.

"Hey, brother! Just finished getting dressed!" he yelled to the kitchen.

Tyrell waved it off as Matthew entered, hair damp and buttoning his shirt. At least Matthew dressed well for the dinner, more than just a t-shirt. Sometimes the t-shirt even had holes. Shaking his head, Tyrell was pleased that Matthew's hook-up with Rosemarie meant he was dressing better.

Tyrell had decided that since it was not supposed to be a blind date, he would don a more casual black and silver button down of his own. Even in more laid-back clothing, Tyrell cut a fine figure. The dress shirt flattered his pumped, well-muscled chest, and the short sleeves rolled up right at his bicep muscles, framing them nicely.

Matthew began placing condiments and plates around the table in the dining area just off the kitchen. The dark, walnut table was a newer purchase since they had moved in together, and Rosemarie was always up for entertaining at home to show it off. He eyed Tyrell as he slipped a fourth plate onto the table.

"Shit, man." Tyrell rolled his deep brown eyes to the ceiling in an exaggerated manner.

"It's not really a date. It's not a setup, I promise. Just invited some friends over for dinner, that's all." Matthew's sheepish look returned.

"I knew that's what this was about."

Tyrell tried to sound mad, but in truth, he wasn't. If he didn't want to be here, get set up, then he would've just turned down the invite. He was more of a "grab life for all you can" type of guy, so why not meet more people? If he met enough people, maybe he'd luck out like Matthew and meet *the one*.

"And if you don't want her number, no biggie," Matthew said, matter-of-factly, as if he read Tyrell's mind. "I'm sure you have a whole pile of other numbers from your time at the gym this week."

He wasn't wrong. "Fine, but the food better be excellent," Tyrell quipped, his smile tugging at the side of his mouth. Matthew threw a napkin at him.

"When is it not? I'm lucky she cooks the healthy stuff, or I'd have to go to the gym a lot more." Matthew shook his head, and Tyrell's booming laugh echoed in the dining room.

Dinner went well, even if Tyrell didn't feel sparks at the young woman Rosemarie invited over. Evidently, she was a server who used to work with Rosemarie. She was a cute blonde named Sal, short for nothing she told them. "Just Sal."

"Just Sal" is how Tyrell thought of her for the rest of dinner. She was smart, but very slender and petite — when they stood to leave, she only came up to Tyrell's chest. And she had a way of saying "Oh yeah!" at the beginning of every sentence that grated on Tyrell's nerves. If he met her in a bar, though, he was sure he'd bring her home for the night. But he'd make certain she was on her way home well before morning.

Just Sal didn't seem to like him too much, either. Dinner conversation was polite, even hilarious at times. Her eyes, however, didn't linger on his, and she didn't offer up her phone number when she left. *Probably better that way*, Tyrell told himself. While she may be a fun time, he didn't want to get on anyone's bad side with a date gone wrong. Rosemarie was too good a friend to risk it.

Maybe that was why he had yet to date any of Rosemarie's set-ups. He didn't want Rosemarie to be angry if he broke one of her friend's hearts. And to hear his previous girlfriends tell it, he was a heartbreaker.

He went home alone and made an early night for himself. He had worked overtime the night before, something he had been doing more often. With no girlfriend or wife to come home to, it was just more fun to be on the job. Great for stock-piling money as well. Lately his life was work, sleep, working out, and downtime with his beat partners or playing video games. He needed something grander to spend his money on than video games.

Tyrell's thoughts drifted to his dinner and the interactions he observed between Matthew and Rosemarie. He *never* thought Matthew would get over his ex and find someone — his brother had been in deep with that woman. And while it took him time, here he was, in this amazing relationship with this incredible woman. Tyrell felt a strange pull in his chest.

He rubbed at it absently, wondering what that sensation was. It went away as he got ready for bed, but once his mind drifted back to his partner's love life, the pulling reappeared. It was a sensation Tyrell had not really experienced before, and it took a moment for him to put a name on it.

As he lay in bed that night, rubbing his chest, it came to him.

Jealousy.

He was jealous of his partner's relationship.

For the first time in his life, Tyrell wanted more than a few dates, more than one-night stands.

Two

The next day, he was up early, met Matthew for lifting and a bit of grilling about Just Sal, then headed out to his shift with the Tustin police department.

October was one of the most beautiful months in Southern California. The leaves didn't quite change as much as one would expect to see in a place like the Midwest; the pines and palms kept their verdant green color year-round. The landscape still resembled a tropical paradise, even as the temperatures became more temperate. And Tyrell loved the more temperate weather. Aside from a chance of much-needed rain, it was paradise.

He tended to sweat excessively in the summer and early fall, even in the short sleeve uniform. What with the dark navy polyester fabric, the bullet-proof vest, and his undershirt, plus the long dark pants, thick socks, and heavy boots, there was just not enough air conditioning to keep him cool. August was like a sauna, and he welcomed the cooler weather of fall like an old friend he had missed.

Even the sun looked different in autumn, close to Halloween. Sunset was more colorful, filling the skies in shades of pinks, purples, and oranges, and if Tyrell were a painting man, he'd cover canvases in those sunset hues. It made the car ride to the station calming and enjoyable.

And those two emotions were ones he needed before stepping out into the busy streets in uniform for the night shift. The heat of the summer may have left with the season, but the crazies and criminals remained. And nothing was worse that a night full of crazy.

When he arrived at the station, it was already buzzing with the end of swing shift, calls holding, and officers racing around. Evidently, a random traffic stop led to a decently sized drug bust, and that meant other calls held as officers worked the drug arrests. After briefing, Tyrell hit the ground running.

His first call involved a transient trying to break into an office building off Newport Road — an easy enough call. Tyrell was able to help the guy out, calling a contact at a nearby shelter and received a "Thank you, officer" for his efforts. Not a bad start to his night. He tugged at his vest, so it didn't shift around on his chest, and started to pull back onto Newport when he was flagged down by a woman who wanted to know if her dad was in an accident.

"What?" Tyrell had no idea who her dad was. Why did people think cops were psychic?

"He got off work an hour ago and still isn't home. Have you responded to any accidents?" The woman's voice rose to a high-pitched panic.

Tyrell checked his screen. He hadn't responded to any accidents, and nothing appeared on the onboard computer, and he told the woman as much.

"Well, how can I find him, officer?"

Tyrell sighed. He wondered what people believed police actually did for a living. An information booth, he was not.

"Ma'am, you can try calling the local hospitals, if you're worried about his health. Other than that, you'd have to wait 72 hours to report him missing."

This news was obviously not what she wanted to hear, and she exhaled in an angry breath. She gave him a curt "Thanks, officer" and walked back to her car.

Tyrell shook his head but couldn't really complain. It was only 11 pm, and the night was relatively calm. No calls holding on his computer — those had started to clear up — no more crazies on the street flagging him down, and his only interactions so far were mild. No reports, no arrests. Tyrell settled in for a boring evening on patrol.

Until an open-top, raised Jeep Wrangler blew through the stoplight. And Officer Tyrell Blaser lit it up.

The Jeep Wrangler continued racing down Newport Road, with Tyrell in hot pursuit, until he watched the driver flip their head up to the rear-view mirror. Then the brake lights flicked on as the Jeep finally began to slow, and the driver pulled the monster truck against the curb.

Whipping behind the car before the driver made any sudden moves, Tyrell typed his location into the computer as he flicked the spotlight onto the Jeep — a maroon-ish red, Tyrell mentally noted — and tapped on his body camera. As he approached the Jeep, he kept one hand on his service weapon. When a driver is treating the main road as their own, personal drag strip, Tyrell never knew what type of person would be behind the wheel. Better safe than sorry.

What he did not expect was a strikingly beautiful woman in shorts and a tank top (*she has to be freezing*, Tyrell noted), and mascara tear stains on her cheeks. She kept flipping her head behind her and to her rear-view mirror, as though she expected someone else to join her, and Tyrell kept a keen eye to the right. He would allow no surprise visitors on this traffic stop, and his fingers remained tight around his pistol grip.

"Ma'am, do you know why I pulled you over?" he asked, looking up at the driver.

Since the Jeep was lifted, her head was just above his. No door separated them, as the Jeep's soft-top cover was absent, and he could watch every move she made, which made him feel safer in the traffic stop. And he also didn't miss the panicky expression on her stunning face. Her hazel brown eyes were full of tears, her mascara smudged heavily around her eyes, raccoon-style, and smeared all the way down her cheeks.

Tyrell was immediately on alert. This was more than a traffic stop.

"Yeah, no, um, yeah, I do," her voice shook as much as her hands. "I didn't stop for that light. I thought I could make it. I was already going fast, so I didn't want to stop."

"Do you have any idea how fast you were going?" Tyrell took his hand off his weapon and pulled his ticket book out of his breast pocket and clicked the pen attached.

"No, Officer, I'm sorry," she pleaded.

Turning her attention to him, she finally pulled her eyes off her rear-view mirror and faced him directly. Tyrell had to work to keep his eyes on her face and off her full breasts that were at eye-level. The tight tank top did not help him at all. And he wasn't wearing his sunglasses to hide his eyes. She leaned forward to look at him directly and gave him an even better view of her breasts that apparently lacked a bra.

He cursed himself for not keeping it together and refocused. If she thought to use her assets to get out of a ticket, she was so wrong.

"Ma'am, have you had anything to drink tonight?" he asked.

Her behavior was abnormal, not a typical traffic stop, and while she didn't scream "drunk" or even high, something was going on. Tyrell was on edge.

"No, no, nothing like that, Officer."

She was also on edge, that was evident. Perhaps she had a warrant? Drugs in the car? Tyrell mentally ticked off his list of what he was going to do on this stop to make sure it cleared and help him figure out what was wrong with this woman. She appeared so desperate, and Tyrell entertained a moment of concern before putting his officer persona back into place.

"License, registration, and proof of insurance, please," he requested.

He watched as she flicked her eyes to her rear-view mirror again before reaching for the glove box. Keeping a wary eye on the woman, he gave another quick glance to the right again. *Who was she looking for?*

She held her paperwork out to him, her slender arm a perfect shade of copper, her nails coated in chipped red nail polish. For someone as breathtaking as this woman, the smeared mascara, the panic, the chipped nails only heightened Tyrell's caution for this stop. Something was not right, and his intuition told him it was more than drinking or drugs. This was much larger. Tyrell waited for the hammer to come down.

"Ma'am, wait here," he told her, and returned to his black and white.

As he sat in the driver's seat to run her license, he left the door open and kept one leg extended from the car in case he needed to jump out and chase her.

His eyes were on the computer when the late-model, sporty sedan careened down Newport, swerved toward where his car and hers were parked. Tyrell managed to pull his leg in as the sedan slammed past his open car door, peeling it from the vehicle, and side-swiped the Jeep with a heavy crunching sound.

"Holy fuck!" Tyrell yelled as the car picked up speed, racing off in a cloud of dirt.

He was immediately on his radio, calling for support and reading off the license plate before jumping out of his car to check on the Jeep driver. As he rushed to her, he sent up a silent *THANK GOD* he pulled his leg into the car; otherwise he'd be taking an early medical retirement.

A large, scraping dent extended from the rear passenger wheel well over the gap of the driver's door to the front wheel well. The woman, whose name on her license read Vivienne Maya, shook in her seat, crying.

"Ma'am, are you Ok?" Tyrell's surprised wariness came through his tone.

Vivienne nodded as the tears continued to streak her face. Tyrell wanted to jump into his car and give chase — he needed to catch this crazed driver. *Who was this guy? Was this what the woman kept looking for in her rear-view?*

Tyrell took two steps toward his black and white then pulled himself to a stop. The driver's door lay like a turtle on its back less than a foot from the woman's Jeep. He would not give chase; he'd be fired in a heartbeat if he took off in a cop car that was missing the driver's side door.

Swinging around to the direction the sedan sped off, Tyrell glowered down the street, then collected himself before returning to the woman. His traffic offender-turned-victim needed his attention more. The radio squawked over and over as different officers radioed in their part of the chase. Time to let his brothers in blue catch the perp. He had to figure out what the hell just happened and assist the poor woman in the Jeep.

Three

Tilting his head back to his radio, he called for an ambulance and not one, but two, tows. His sergeant would not be happy at the damage to the 23 car, which would be a whole other set of paperwork to fill out. His radio squawked that the chase may be over, as they lost the car in a neighborhood to the south.

"Fuck," he said to himself as he walked over to the woman in the Jeep.

Ms. Vivienne Maya had not moved. Her hands were still at ten and two on her steering wheel, and she had not stopped shivering. She was in shock, and Tyrell had to move quickly.

Rushing back to his car, he popped the trunk and pulled a plain wool blanket from the back. He ran to the Jeep and, explaining what he was doing in the most soothing voice he could muster, he reached across her stomach and unclipped her seat belt.

"Hey, hey, step down to me, Ok?" he crooned, like he was speaking to an injured animal. In a way, he was.

Vivienne moved her leg to step out of the car and stumbled, unable to keep her balance. Tyrell caught her as she fell, and as he did so, he noted her skin had gone from a coppery shade to a sickly pale hue. Shock was setting in.

He wrapped her in the blanket and lay her on the ground in front of her car. Lifting her legs, he put them on his lap and radioed again.

"Where's that bus? The vic is in shock," he said, keeping his voice level. He didn't need to have Ms. Maya panic as well.

"Two minutes out," dispatch reported.

Tyrell returned his attention to the woman shivering in the blanket, patting at her ankles.

"Hey, hey, ma'am, you're all good. The ambulance will be here in a minute, and they will take good care of you." He hoped his voice was as reassuring as he thought it sounded.

While he didn't want her to over-exert herself — he didn't need her crashing on him — what he did need was information about that speeding car.

"Ma'am, Ms. Maya? Can you tell me a little bit about what happened tonight? Do you know who the driver of that sedan was?" Tyrell asked in his crooning tone.

"My ex," Vivienne croaked out. She rotated her head to look down her nose at where he sat by her feet. Her two-word answer told him more than she realized.

"Are you keeping my feet elevated? Did the car hit me or something?"

She didn't sound panicked or concerned at all. In fact, her voice was resigned, and Tyrell didn't like it.

"No, ma'am, not from what I could see. Do you feel like you have an injury anywhere?"

She lifted her hand awkwardly and brushed at her pasty cheek. "My head hurts the most. I have a headache."

Her unbelievable calm at the whole situation sparked a nugget of concern with Tyrell. *Was she used to this? Why didn't she seem surprised?*

"Well, the paramedics will be able to help you with that," he responded as he heard the sirens wail in the distance. Flicking his gaze around the front of the car, he saw the red and white flashing lights approach.

"I'm just going to flag them to us. I'm not going anywhere," he reassured her again before setting her feet on the ground and standing in the light of the oncoming ambulance.

The paramedics leapt out of the bus, pulling gear and the gurney out of the back with a singular focus. They bent over Vivienne, working their life-saving magic and asking their series of questions. Tyrell left her in their capable hands as he picked his way over the debris to the 44 black and white that followed the ambulance to his location.

Tony Sepulveda stepped out, looking formidable in his vest and uniform and scowling expression that only made him appear even more intimidating. He did not relish losing a perp, and when he heard the car chased ended with no arrest, he was pissed, taking it personally even if he wasn't part of the chase. His dark brown hair stood up on end as he walked to Tyrell.

"What the hell happened here? You Ok, brother?"

"Hey, brother. Yeah, but my vic's in shock. Seems she's got an ex who isn't happy about being an ex, and he tried to drive her off the road. Sideswiped her car and mine when I pulled her over for a traffic stop. I don't have all the deets, but I'll jump in the wagon and go to the hospital with her." His eyes flicked to his damaged car. "Obviously, I won't be driving there."

"Yeah, brother. I'm on deck to monitor the scene, wait for the investigators and the tow, then get you when you're done with the vic. What a bucket, eh?"

Tony's lips pulled to one side in a grimace at the mess of a scene. It would take hours to clean up and piles of paperwork to complete. Tyrell nodded in agreement. The whole night turned into a bucket. And they didn't even get the guy responsible. That knowledge hung over Tyrell. The only bright spot was perhaps the vic could tell them where to find the driver of the sedan, and he told Tony as much.

"Yeah, if she's not too bad off, we may get what we need from her. Good luck, brother," Tony waved him off as the investigators pulled up in an unmarked car.

Tyrell returned to the paramedics where they were placing Vivienne on the gurney. A clear oxygen mask covered most her face, and the blanket was still tucked around her. Only one arm was exposed where the EMT had started a saline line to get fluids into her. They rolled her into the bus, and the long-haired EMT gestured at Tyrell.

"Are you joining us?" she asked.

He dipped his head and followed the paramedic into the rear of the ambulance. The other EMT slammed the doors shut, and Tyrell had to squint at the bright lights overhead. He waited patiently for the EMT to finish her round of questions, making sure Vivienne was not in immediate danger, and place an ice pack on her clammy forehead.

Vivienne appeared coherent enough, responding to the paramedic's questions. Once she was satisfied, the EMT shifted her alert brown eyes to Tyrell.

"I think she's stable for now. And talkative enough. I assume you have a bunch of questions for her. Go ahead," she said curtly.

Tyrell moved his intense gaze to the beautiful woman strapped to the bed.

"Are you up for some questions?" Tyrell asked, keeping his voice calm and level amid the sirens and speeding vehicle.

Vivienne tipped her head to the side to better view him, nodding yes.

"Ok, then," Tyrell continued, pulling his notebook and pen out of his breast pocket. "Can you tell me what happened tonight?"

Vivienne cleared her throat, her voice sounding almost numb as she spoke, like her mind was suffering from the same shock as her body.

"I broke up with him, like, a month or so ago?" she began her story, her voice hollow through the oxygen mask. Tyrell held up his hand.

"Does he have a name?"

"Jason. Jason Kane," she answered.

Tyrell noted the name in his book. "Cane with a "C"?" he asked.

She shook her head. He made another note and lifted his calm gaze to Vivienne. "Ok, go on."

"Jason, he's not anything big. He thinks he is, but he's just so, um, average, right?"

Tyrell inclined his head. He was familiar with the type of man she described. He had arrested more than his fair share at every family function and event known to man, usually as a 10-16, domestic disturbance. His pen scratched as he wrote, trying to write legibly in the rear of the jouncing ambulance.

"He thought that, since we were dating, he could tell me where to go, who to be friends with, what to wear, and I'm not that person. We had several fights, like loud, yelling fights. I'm surprised the neighbors didn't call the cops, really. But he hit me once. ONCE," she emphasized, lifting her head off the gurney.

The EMT clicked her tongue and placed a hand on Vivienne's shoulder to have her recline back on the pad and pulled off the oxygen mask. Vivienne dropped her head onto the flat pillow, inhaling deeply.

"I left him, and he didn't like that. Texting me, stalking me, social media stalking, contacting my friends, all that. I totally cut him off, and he just got madder and madder. But I didn't think he would go this far. I didn't think he was that guy, you know?"

"Yeah, I know," Tyrell answered, and he did. Even the best people can become monsters when pushed too far.

"Tonight, I got home from the gym. I sell insurance. Super exciting, right? And I have a flexible schedule, for the most part. Today was end of the month, so I didn't get to go early in the day, so I went after work. I guess he's been watching me, my schedule, and got pissed that I was not home from work when I was supposed to be."

She shook her head at the memory, her hair catching the interior light and shaking in a flow of earthy colors. Tyrell was momentarily mesmerized.

"I was shocked, and I got mad. I won't lie. I mean, we aren't dating, and who is he to watch my schedule like that? And I told him that. No, I yelled it. Right in his face. Told him he was a worthless loser who needed to get a life and he lifted his hand and threatened to punch me. I mean, if I kept my mouth shut —"

"Whoa!" Tyrell interrupted. "Don't even go there. It's a free country, and unless you hit him first, he has no right to put his hands on you. You have a voice; you get to use it. Don't let some guy dictate what you can or can't say, especially if he tries to do it with his fists."

Vivienne bit her lip at his outburst, the support for her actions making her feel better than the saline in her arm. It's hard to stand up against someone, and she said that out loud. Tyrell chuckled, his vest vibrating with his chest.

"Look at who you're talking to," Tyrell smiled as he spoke, his teeth brilliant against his attractive face under the lights of the ambulance, and Vivienne's breath caught.

The last thing she needed was to fall for the handsome hero cop, especially after exiting a potentially abusive relationship. Those stories never had a happy ending, she knew. The EMT noted the reaction and pressed her fingers under Vivienne's jaw to check her blood pressure.

"Yeah, I get that. Thank you for that. So, after he threatened me, I started yelling for someone to call the police. He left, and I thought that was the end of it, but after I got home from a girl's night to rant to a friend, he was waiting for me in the driveway of my apartment complex. His stupid little sedan in my parking spot, but I didn't want any problems. I decided to drive back to my friend's, spend the night, whatever. Janelle would be Ok with it, but he followed me. He kept doing that thing where he'd get up close on my bumper, you know?" She used her hands to show how close their bumpers would be, then dropped her arms to the gurney.

"I had to bail, so I turned onto Newport, and now I'm going like, I dunno, 60? I'm trying to lose him, but he's right there. He got caught at that light I blew through."

Vivienne's voice dropped with her eyes. She was admitting to breaking the law to the cop who pulled her over. That would be a huge ticket and a day at online driving school, so her insurance didn't skyrocket. *Oh, the irony,* she thought.

She lifted her soft brown eyes to his. "That's why I ran the light. I am sorry for that. But I thought I'd be Ok once you pulled me over. I was freaking *grateful* for getting pulled over, can you believe that?"

"Yes, I can," Tyrell responded with full honesty as he wrote as fast as he could to keep up with her narrative.

"Anyway, so am I getting a ticket for speeding and running that light? How much is that ticket, do you know?" Her tone was flat, expectant, and Tyrell had to bite back a laugh.

He flicked his eyes to the EMT, who sagely kept her focus on Vivienne. The other EMT called out that they were pulling into the ER bay.

"We will talk about that more later. We're here. Let's get you settled. Then I'm going to need information on the ex."

Four

Tyrell's radio chattered with information regarding the Jeep, his patrol car, and the continued search for the late model sedan. He radioed in that the vic had arrived at the hospital and once she was cleared by the doctors, he would question her more about the perp. Tony made sure to bitch about the extra paperwork since Blaser got his car wrecked, and Tyrell laughed to himself as he walked to the curtain of the vic's hospital bed.

The doctor stepped out, leaving the curtain open a crack. He informed Tyrell that the shock was wearing off, and the vic would be released shortly.

"Can I go in to ask her some questions?"

The doctor held his hand to the curtain. "Yep, she should be good."

Tyrell stepped around the pale blue curtain to the stunning woman on the uncomfortable-looking bed, her eyes closed against the world. He paused a moment to admire her — she resembled a photograph in a magazine, her hair a wild river of waves against her now, more healthy-looking skin. As a courtesy, he cleared his throat, and she opened her eyelids.

"Hey, Officer," she said, her gentle smile creasing the edges of her eyes. Tyrell could not stop himself from smiling back.

"Hey, you. How are you feeling, Ms. Maya?" he asked lightly as he reached for his notepad and pen again. Time to get back to work.

"Better, thanks to you and the EMTs. I just feel stupid for getting myself in this situation. I'm not that person, you know?"

"Well, that's why I have a job. We never know when life will get crazy on us."

"So, I overheard you talking with the doctor. More questions? About Jason, right?"

He pointed a strong finger at her, then tapped his pen against his pad. "You got it. You gave me all the info on what happened, but now we need to find the guy."

"He got away? In his crappy car?" Disbelief and a nuance of horror skittered across her features, and Tyrell was impelled to console her.

"The cops gave a good chase, but they lost him. That's why we need you. The more information you can give us on him, the better chance we will have of catching him."

Vivienne pursed her lips. "Yeah, ok, where do you want me to start?"

"I got his name. I have a picture here," he pulled out his phone, showing her the Cal photo ID. "Who is this guy?"

"Yeah, that's Jason Kane, the guy in the sedan."

"Any aliases?" Tyrell put the phone away and clicked his pen, poised to write.

"Not that he told me. I only know him as Jason Kane."

Scritch-scratch went the pen on the paper, surprisingly loud in the din of the hospital. Vivienne noted he was left-handed.

"I'm a lefty, too," she told him abruptly.

"I'm sorry?" he asked, lifting his eyes to her. Vivienne raised her left hand.

"Lefty? Me too," she smiled at him, and he smiled back.

"Yeah, I have to be careful not to get those really wet pens or my notes are a streaky mess."

For a reason she couldn't put a finger on, this answer struck Vivienne as hilarious, and she burst into a fit of giggles. Her laugh was infectious, and Tyrell laughed along with her.

"I'm sorry. I'm distracting you," she apologized.

"Nope. With everything that happened tonight, it probably feels good to laugh."

His own smile reached his intense onyx eyes, and Vivienne's heart fluttered. *It's just the attention of a man in uniform,* she told herself. *Don't read into it.*

"What does this ex look like? Anything the pic doesn't tell us?" Tyrell got back to business.

"He's so average," Vivienne used the same wording as she did earlier. "He's around six feet tall, brown hair, brown eyes, average weight, maybe two hundred pounds? Oh, he wears a lot of Orange County College stuff — he played baseball for them. His moment in the spotlight, and he can't let it go."

Tyrell made notes to check with the college to see if the perp had a violent history there, then continued.

"And his job? Where does he work?"

"I'm not sure," she confessed. "He does handyman work for his brother, who's a realtor, and then for some people in the area. But he does most of it under the table, I think, and not just here in Tustin."

"Is that your way of saying if we can't find him at home or at his brother's, he could be hiding anywhere?"

Vivienne bit her lip and nodded dejectedly. "He knows so many people, friends, family, college, and a lot of them are not on the level, I don't think. I can give you a list of where he might be, like where he frequents? But that's about it."

Tyrell nodded placatingly, assuring her that any information was valuable. Especially since the jackass hit a cop car — that BOLO and subsequent hit-and-run warrant would go out hot tonight.

Vivienne gave Tyrell a short list of where Jason could be hiding out, then gave him her contact numbers so he could follow up. She promised to try to get more details for him when she got home. After he noted this information, he pulled a small card out of his notebook.

"Here, this is all my contact information," Tyrell told her. "If you remember anything else, see him anywhere, or have any problems, you call me right away. If it's an emergency, he comes back violent, call 911. Do not wait. Do not try to reason with him. I don't want him actually hitting you the next time, especially with his car. Guys like this, in my experience, are unreasonable and tend to escalate."

Vivienne took the card in her slender grasp, eyeing the lettering on the card.

"Officer Tyrell Blaser. Well, it's nice to have a name to put to the face."

The nurse came in with her release paperwork, and Vivienne signed it all. She made to sit up, and Tyrell hurried to help her rise from the bed.

"You going to be Ok?" he asked, his voice filled with concern. He let his hands linger on her back and arm.

"I think so. What time is it?" she asked.

Tyrell glanced at his watch. "2:30 am. Do you have a ride?"

Vivienne burst out laughing. At Tyrell's quizzical expression, she straightened.

"At 2:30 in the morning? I could ask you the same. You got a cop coming to pick you up?"

Tyrell's head fell forward. He radioed to Tony telling him the vic was being released. The radio squawked that he'd finish up paperwork and be on his way to get Tyrell.

"Now, who's getting you?" he asked. "Do you have someone who can pick you up?"

Vivienne shook her head as they approached the waiting area of the hospital.

"No, It's too late. I'll have to call a car from my ride app to get me."

"No parents in the area?"

Vivienne shook her head again. "It's late, and I don't want to worry them."

She tapped on her phone, and her app told her a ride would arrive in fifteen minutes. Vivienne settled in to wait. Tyrell sat in the plastic, gray chair next to her.

"Are you going to wait with me?" she asked.

It felt strange to make small talk with a cop in full uniform. Great eye candy, though, and she was feeling well enough to appreciate the view. His posture was perfectly straight, a result of extra girth from his vest, the deep blue of the uniform flattering him in the harsh waiting room lights. The handcuffs and gun on his hip added an element of dangerous excitement to his handsome resolve.

"I have to wait, too, so I might as well enjoy the company until then." Tyrell flashed his renowned smile at her, hoping to receive a dazzling one from her in return. He was not disappointed.

"You didn't answer my question from earlier," she said, her sly gaze softening her face, and it mesmerized him. Tyrell's chest clenched with a rush of excitement, and he worked to tamp it down and control himself as he responded.

"What question?" He couldn't recall what she was talking about.

"Aren't you going to write me a ticket? Since I ran a light and was speeding?"

Vivienne couldn't believe her audacity. Was she really flirting with a cop in the hospital to get out of a ticket for traffic violations she was admitting to? She took a sidelong glance at Officer Blaser — his smooth skin, his strong presence, that foxy uniform, those bedroom eyes that she wanted to lose herself in — yeah, she was totally flirting.

And he knew it. Tyrell gave her a wry grin in return. There it was. If he didn't already have her digits, she'd have given them to him now. Even in the thick of it all, he still had his game.

But for some reason, his heart fluttered at her flirting, and his blood rushed to his head, making him dizzy. This wasn't just typical flirting, like getting numbers from girls at the gym. This was something more. He was certain of it.

"Since you were under duress, ma'am," he told her in his most serious cop tone, "I think I will make an exception this time."

She let her fingertips touch his strong hand. "Thank you, Officer."

The ride share car, a minuscule white hatchback, arrived with a minute to spare. Tyrell made sure the driver matched the app description and then opened the door, helping Vivienne into the back of the vehicle. He leaned into the car before closing it.

"Again, Ms. Maya. If you need anything, call me or 911 if it's an emergency. Don't leave anything to chance." His stern, authoritative tone had returned.

"Of course. And thank you again, Officer Blaser. I appreciate everything you've done for me."

Tyrell gave her a curt nod and shut the rear passenger door. He knocked twice on the roof of the car, and the driver pulled away from the hospital bay curb and out into the darkness of early morning.

Glancing at his watch, Tyrell noted that it was after 3 am, and Officer Sepulveda should have arrived. He grabbed his phone and sent a quick text asking after his ride. Tony's text was full of humorous innuendo:

I've been here, in the lot, watching you ogle over the hot vic. Now get in the car, we have paperwork to fill out.

Tyrell scanned the parking lot and noted the black and white parked at the front of the emergency entrance. He hiked over to the squad car and got in as Tony laid into him.

"Wow, you don't waste any time, do you? Do you have a date set up already? Not that I blame you, the vic's a hottie!" Tony leered from the driver's seat. Tyrell gave him a decently strong punch to the arm.

"Cut it. Nothing like that. Just helping her out."

"Oh, I'm sure that was helping her a lot. Helping her out on a date? Out of her clothes? Into your —"

"All right already!" Tyrell shouted. Tony backed off, the leering smile still plastered on his face.

"Ok but get your head in the game. I am not filling out all that paperwork on my own. That was your TC after all!"

Tyrell laughed as he shook his head. "Just drive, asshole."

Five

Between getting back to the station and completing the paperwork, Tyrell caught an hour of overtime before heading home. He couldn't recall the last time he felt so wiped out. Thursdays were his rest days, fortunately, which meant he could sleep in since he didn't have to hit the gym. And he slept hard. He woke seven hours later, groggy and disoriented. He took a minute to get his bearings before leaving the sanctuary of his bed and gearing up for another night of work.

He just hoped that his car made it through the night. He didn't want to fill out another giant stack of paperwork over another wrecked car. After the bucket of crap from the previous night, tonight had to be better. *Gotta think positive,* he told himself.

He got to the station right at 8:00 pm, ready to don his uniform, vest, belt, and be in briefing by 8:30. As he left the locker room, headed for briefing, the front desk officer hollered for him.

"Blaser!" Officer Carson's voice carried through the station.

Tyrell spun on his toe in an agile move and approached the counter.

"Yeah, brother?" Why was he needed at the front desk?

Carson flicked his eyes across the room. "You got a visitor, brother."

Tyrell turned his chiseled profile and peered over the cheap plastic chairs in reception to find the striking Vivienne Maya standing off to the side, a large plastic container in her hands. She looked much healthier, her make-up and hair almost perfect. His smile lit up his whole face, and Vivienne gave him a relieved smile in return. Tyrell stepped around the chairs to meet her.

"Ms. Maya! To what do I owe this pleasure?"

While his words were standard courtesy, the warmth in his voice was clear. Vivienne let her eyes roam up and down his muscular, uniformed body before answering. He knew his attractive physique showed off his uniform well, and he shifted to give her a good view as he waited for her response.

"Officer Blaser. Two things. One, I went home and looked up some addresses and phone numbers of the names I gave you last night, where you might find Jason?"

She held out a piece of notebook paper, and Tyrell nodded, taking it from her. He was impressed at how quickly she operated. She seemed a pro-active person, and he admired the trait.

"Are you going to get your Jeep fixed soon?" he asked, genuinely interested. He didn't want her driving around in a busted-up car. She deserved better than that.

"Yeah, my dad knows a guy so I'm taking it in first thing in the morning. It's still drivable, but looks ugly, and I don't want to wreck the tires. He said he can get it done fast, so I'm borrowing my mom's car until it's done. No biggie."

"And the second thing?" he asked.

Vivienne held out the plastic container. "This may be retro, but I made cookies for you and your boys in blue for helping me out last night. You went above and beyond, and I just wanted to say thank you."

Tyrell took the container and peeked under the lid. Chocolate chip. Who didn't love chocolate chip? And cookies were his kryptonite.

"This will mean extra time at the gym for certain," he told her. "These look delicious. Do I have to share?"

Vivienne winked at him. She leaned in close, whispering conspiratorially, and the musky scent of her perfume filled his senses.

"Well, if you keep them for yourself, I won't tell anyone."

"Ah, Ms. Maya, you are dangerous indeed," he joked, but stayed close to her.

"Especially since I almost got you hit by a car last night!" she joked back. "This was the least I could do!"

Her face grew serious, and she placed a light hand on Tyrell's arm. Her palm seemed to sear his skin. It took all of his concentration to keep his mind on what she was saying.

"But really," she continued, "thank you for everything. I really appreciate it."

Tyrell bowed his head to her. "You are more than welcome, Ms. Maya."

She let her soft brown eyes gaze into his own intense face and, eyeing his uniformed figure once more, turned and exited the station.

As he watched her sashay through the double doors, he both admired the curvaceous backside and sensed he may have missed an important opportunity.

Racing back to the locker room, Tyrell placed the cookies in his locker. Before he left them, he popped open the rubbery lid and slipped out several. One for him and some to share, of course. As he removed his hand from the container, he felt a slip of paper on top of the cookies. He pulled that out as well.

He shoved one crumbly piece in his mouth and read the card as he stepped away from his locker. The message on the card stopped him.

Want to meet for coffee sometime? Followed by her digits.

Opportunity reclaimed. Tyrell smiled to himself, mouth full of sweet cookie, and resumed his walk to the briefing room. He was late, there was no denying that, and there would be some catcalls by the cops who saw him chatting with Vivienne in reception. And he really didn't care.

He was not disappointed. Some of the guys even applauded, but Tyrell lifted his head to acknowledge the teasing and hide any embarrassment. He raised a hand as if the accolades were welcome and sat next to Tony, passing him a cookie treat.

"You bake?" Sepulveda asked disbelievingly.

"Naw, brother," Tyrell said, unable to keep the sly grin off his lips. "A gift from a thankful vic."

"Oh, ho ho!" Tony laughed under his breath. "I think I know which vic. That hottie brunette from last night? The one that came to the station tonight?"

Tyrell didn't answer and gave Tony a knowing look.

"I'm surprised she didn't ask you out," Tony admitted.

Again, Tyrell remained silent. If word got out that a vic asked him out the very next day, that would not be well received. Better to keep it on the down low until he saw where things went with Vivienne. And he might not even call her anyway, so why bother?

But he would call her. He knew that the minute he saw her standing like a sexy, mythical goddess in reception.

Six

Tyrell waited an obligatory three days before calling her. He didn't want to appear overly eager. Since he had Sunday off and didn't put in for overtime, so he decided it was time to risk it. He punched her numbers into his phone, and she picked up on the second ring.

"Hello?"

"Hey, Ms. Maya. It's Officer Blaser." He sounded so formal. This was his first time calling a vic out for a date, and he wasn't sure of the protocol.

"Hello, Officer Blaser." Tyrell heard the humor in her voice over the speaker. "To what do I owe this pleasure?" she asked, repeating his words from the night before. He couldn't help but smile into the phone.

"I got your message in the cookies. I think coffee is a great idea. I know it's last minute, but are you free today?"

"Hmm, let me check my schedule. I have laundry and food prep on deck, but if I skip binging on TV, I can meet you," she joked. Tyrell's insides ignited.

"Where would you like to meet?"

"There's a coffeehouse off Newport and Sanders, if you want to meet there? Waterhouse Coffees?"

"That sounds like a great idea. Would you be able to meet in an hour?" An hour? *Crap*, he thought. That *did* sound too eager.

"I can do that," she replied. "Oh, and Officer Blaser?"

"Yes, ma'am," he responded.

"It's Vivienne. I think if we're going to meet for coffee, we should be on a first name basis."

A deep chuckle rolled from Tyrell's chest. The woman kept him hopping, that was certain. "Tyrell," he told her. "My name's Tyrell, Vivienne."

"Nice to meet you, Tyrell," she told him in that slightly dry voice. "I would love to meet you in an hour."

The phone clicked off, and butterflies frolicked in his stomach. It was the first time in a long while since he felt this much excitement over meeting a woman. Tyrell raced to the bathroom to shower off his workout and get ready for his date.

The coffeehouse was surprisingly packed when Tyrell arrived, several dangling ghost and pumpkin cut-outs adding to the crowded effect. Fortunately, his height allowed him to peer over the heads of the patrons grasping for their caffeine fix and find a familiar, tortoise-shell head standing near the pickup counter. He waited patiently to put in his own drink order, then pushed past the crowd to get Vivienne's attention.

She saw him as he picked his way through the throng of coffee drinkers. His height, glossy skin, and handsome features were impossible to miss, and he attracted the attention of many other women in the coffeehouse. Vivienne smiled to herself, feeling lucky that this gorgeous man was on a date with her.

Her coffee order slid across the counter just as Tyrell reached her. Standing on tippy-toes, she kissed his cheek when he appeared. His smile consumed his entire face at her bold move.

"Did you get to order yet?" she asked as she grabbed the blue and white cup from the counter.

"Yeah, but it may take a while. Man, this place is packed!" He swiveled his head around to make his point.

"They have some sort of secret menu. You ever been here before?"

Tyrell shook his head. "Naw, I'm a cop. We get our coffee at 7-11."

Vivienne giggled at his joke, her smile warming him all the more.

"But really," he continued, "I don't drink that much coffee. Other cops do. Christ, my beat partner Matthew is trying to make it the new water."

Vivienne couldn't stop grinning as he spoke. A funny cop as well! His personality somehow shone more brightly than his handsome face. She understood why women liked him — he was addictively likable. She was certain he was still friends with all his exes.

That notion brought her around to her own problematic ex, a thought she did not want plaguing her coffee date with the sexy police officer. Clearing her throat, she fixed her gaze on his deep black-brown eyes, willing herself to get lost in those depths.

A hand placed Tyrell's order on the counter, a cold, frothy drink spilling over the lip of the cup — so not what Vivienne expected. This man was full of surprises.

Since the inside of the coffeehouse was stiflingly crowded, and the weather outside was cool but sunny, Tyrell placed a gentle hand on her back, and they walked to the outdoor deck area and settled at a small table. From their location, they had a decent view of the sidewalk, but bushes blocked most of the busy road, creating a sanctuary for the coffee drinkers.

Tyrell held up his cup in a "cheers" motion, and Vivienne reciprocated, tapping her cup against his.

"To traffic stops," Tyrell mused, winning a face-splitting smile from Vivienne.

"And to not getting a ticket for it!" she finished.

They took a moment to sip their drinks and enjoy the scenery before picking up the conversation.

Most of Vivienne's initial questions focused on Tyrell as a police officer, a line of questioning he was familiar with. Yes, he loved his job. He had been a cop for seven years. Yes, the vest got hot in the summer. Yes, he had fired his gun. No, he had not killed anyone on the job, yet.

Vivienne kept turning the questions to him, and Tyrell tried to guess why.

"Don't you want to talk about your line of work at all?"

Vivienne rolled her light brown eyes dramatically. "My 'line of work'? Not really. I mean, compared to what you do, hell, compared to anything, insurance is the least exciting job in the world."

Tyrell wasn't sure he could disagree. "So, no exciting stories at all? No crazy claims?"

Most people did not want to hear any insurance stories, and Vivienne tipped her head to the side, grateful for his attempt. Tyrell noticed she had an amazing way of smiling with her eyes. He wanted to see more of it.

"Ok, so we did have one case — " she started.

"I knew you had to have something!"

"It's raining one night, if I can remember it. And this guy, he lives in a duplex, you know, the garage wall is attached to the house next to it? Anyway, he decided he wants to grill his dinner, but not out in the rain."

"Oh, this will not end well," Tyrell predicted, his face wide and engaging. Vivienne again wanted to lose herself in him. Shaking her head slightly, she continued.

"Right? He decided to grill in the garage. Next to his racing fuel."

Tyrell burst out laughing, knowing exactly what would come next. "Ka-boom, am I right?"

Vivienne pointed to her nose. *On the nose,* she thought as she did it, an automatic response. "Yep," she said. "And it caught the garage, and thus the house next door, on fire. We insured the stupid grilling guy. That was a sucky payout, and his rates skyrocketed. I mean, who grills in the garage?"

"Who grills in the garage, right next to racing fuel?" Tyrell finished, and they both chuckled at the idea.

A slight movement from the sidewalk caught the corner of her eye, and her attention wavered from the handsome cop across from her. Tyrell was talking about his gym, something she was interested in since she was fairly demanding with her own workouts. But her eye wouldn't let the distraction go. Tyrell's voice tapered off the harder she looked.

Vivienne leaned past the edge of the table, a conflicted look of horror crossing her features.

Holy shit, she thought to herself. *Is that Jason?*

It couldn't be. He may miss her as his girlfriend, but stalking her like this? That just didn't seem to be him. But after the argument last week and ramming her Jeep, maybe it was. Maybe she didn't know her ex as well as she believed.

"What is it, Vivienne?" Tyrell's voice, and entire demeanor, shifted. No longer light-hearted banter, his tone was serious — a tone you didn't mess around with.

She didn't answer but watched as the guy in the orange baseball cap stepped beyond the bushes. It *was* Jason.

"It's my ex. In his Orange County College cap." Vivienne's voice barely rose above a confused whisper. Tyrell was immediately on alert and stood at the table.

"Where?"

She pointed to where Jason had seemed to slip past the bushes. Tyrell wasted no time and leapt over the slender rail of the decking to the sidewalk and was off running. His speed was shockingly fast, and Vivienne's brain had a crazy twist to marvel that someone could move so fast. He wasn't lying about his workouts. Surely, he would catch her ex.

She rose from the table, leaving their almost-empty drinks behind, and ran down the sidewalk, her stylish, but completely inappropriate-for-running, flats slowing her pace. By the time she got to the end of the bush-lined sidewalk, she found Tyrell scanning the intersection. He wasn't even breathing hard.

"I didn't see him after the bushes. Maybe he had his car parked nearby. Or maybe he doubled back. Are you sure it was him?"

"That freaking hat," she confirmed. "I would know it, and him, anywhere."

Tyrell turned to face her, placing his strong hand on her arm.

"Do we have a stalking issue here? Is this more than just an angry ex situation?"

"I don't know," Vivienne shrugged. "I thought he was just mad that one night. I haven't seen or heard anything from him in the last week."

Tyrell pursed his lips, ferocity emanating from his features. "That may no longer be the case. Why don't we go to the station and have you file a stalking report? I'd like for you to do it today." Concern filled his voice.

And Tyrell knew why. In his seven years on the force, he had seen this scenario play out many times — from men and woman alike. Sometimes a person gets it in their head that the other person belongs to them, that they are destined to be together, and stalking cases rarely end well. A flash of fear rocked through Tyrell, an emotion he wasn't familiar with. He worried about this amazing and beautiful woman. He wanted to know her better, hell, spend his time with her, and he'd not let a crazy, stalking ex hurt her.

But he also knew that filing a stalking report is difficult for many. It's like admitting they were dating or even just friends with someone unstable in a frightening way, that their own judgment was somehow impaired. Tyrell hoped Vivienne was not one of those people.

She wasn't. "You think we should go now? But you aren't on duty."

That was her large concern? His work hours? Tyrell didn't try to hide the small grin that pulled at his lips.

"I'm always working overtime," he told her in an easy tone, trying to lighten the mood a bit. "They would be surprised if I didn't show up today."

It worked, and Vivienne gave him another subtle shrug. "Ok, then. I'll become your overtime."

He took her cool, dainty hand in his larger, warm one and escorted her over the sidewalk to their cars parked outside the coffeehouse. Probably the best overtime he'd ever had, he admitted to himself.

Seven

Their visit to the police station was short and direct, a perk to having a cop personally escort her through the process, Vivienne considered.

He gave her a sweet hug as she departed, and she placed a chaste kiss on his smooth cheek. Tyrell was ecstatic she ventured a kiss — he had worried that the trip to the station would put a damper on her affections, that her ex ruined their day. But maybe it didn't. And he didn't want to leave anything to chance.

"It's Ok if I call you again?" He didn't realize he was holding his breath until she flashed her sly smile at him. Relief smoothed the nervous creases against her eyes.

"I am so glad you asked!" she gushed, almost embarrassed at her reaction.

He opened her car door, and she waved a tanned hand, this time with her manicure on point, a bright green. *Holiday manicure?* he pondered.

As much as he tried to keep his mind on the captivating Vivienne, the cop side of his brain would not let the stalking ex-boyfriend go. If she had no idea he was stalking her, there was a chance he could have been doing it for a long time.

And if he's stalking her while she's on a date, the guy was taking it to the next level. That type of stalking put Vivienne in more danger than she realized. The guy already tried to crash into her on the side of the road. What would stop him from successfully plowing into her when she walked down the street? Across the parking lot of her apartment or gym?

Vacillating between keeping the potential danger to himself, after all he had no solid evidence, or informing her of the danger so she could protect herself, caution won out. After he pulled into his carport at his apartment, he tapped a text on his phone to Vivienne, urging her to be wary that her ex might continue stalking her, and to be careful as she went about her day.

Vivienne sent a heart emoji in return, and Tyrell's chest puffed out. He was surprised at how much he liked this woman, how quickly he seemed to be falling for her.

It was crazy for him to date a vic, to be this invested. The department frowned upon these types of relationships. And they often didn't work for the long run. But there was just something about Vivienne that pulled at his heart, at his groin, at his brain. His thoughts drifted to her and her coppery skin, her marbled hair, her body that was both curvy and tight, and he couldn't stop.

The more his thoughts turned to Vivienne, the more he wanted her. And he decided he had to let her know it.

He snagged another date, this one at Rosemarie's venue, *Wine Time*. The bar provided several elements that Tyrell preferred: a romantic atmosphere, wine to loosen them up, and secluded seating where no exes could peek in while they dined. He told Rosemarie of the recent bouts Vivienne encountered with her ex, and after making a comment about yet another conquest ("It's like you don't even have to try!" she exclaimed, laughing while Tyrell's cheeks heated), she promised that the date would be completely private.

Rosemarie didn't disappoint. Tyrell stepped onto Vivienne's doorstep right at 7:30, sporting a silver and blue fitted button-down shirt that pulled enticingly at his chest and dark denim jeans that followed the curve of his well-muscled ass. He was a vision, and he knew it.

But his own perception of himself dimmed when Vivienne opened the door. She seemed to shine against the light within her apartment. Her hair, shimmering in hues of blonde, brown, black, and silver, was piled on her head in a messy bun, and she wore it like a crown. Her ample breasts pushed against the fabric of her black, sleeveless dress that left little to the imagination. It took all of Tyrell's control not to pull the dress down and lose himself between those coppery globes. With her high-heeled sandals, she was almost as tall as he, the perfect height to take her arm in a gallant gesture. Tyrell held his elbow toward her.

"Shall we, madame?" His voice, silky and suggestive, sent shivers of excitement across Vivienne's spine. She laced her arm through Tyrell's.

"Please," she replied, her own voice husky. Sultry heat passed across Tyrell's features, down his chest to his cock as he led Vivienne to his car.

The purplish lights of *Wine Time* lit up the street as they pulled into the parking lot. Even the brilliant California sun dimmed this late in the season, and it was dark when they arrived. The ornate wooden doors were propped open as an invitation. Tyrell swung one door the rest of the way open to allow Vivienne to enter, and her exquisite face lit up with excitement.

"Where did you find this place?" she asked in awe as he joined her at the hostess station.

"My friend owns it," he admitted. He grinned sheepishly. "We had a meth head storm this place not too long ago, broke a bunch of glass. It was crazy. That was my first time here. This is my second, and she promised a romantic, private night for us."

One slender eyebrow rose on Vivienne's forehead. "Oh, did she now?" Her ruby lips pursed into a sensual smile. "I like the idea of romantic and private," she whispered huskily as the hostess approached the station, menus in hand.

Tyrell gave his name, and the hostess beamed. "We've been expecting you! Come this way."

She led them past the arched doorway into the main room and to the two-person booth, right next to a faux window covered in a heavy, burgundy curtain.

A waitress came to get their drink order, then explained that the evening was taken care of, complete with a special couple's menu created just for them. Tyrell's eyes widened with surprise while Vivienne clapped her hands together lightly.

"Ohh, that is romantic!" she said with glee, turning her gaze on Tyrell. He wanted to explain this was not his idea, but now was not the time. He silently promised to give Rosemarie proper credit later.

The special menu included a surf and turf with asparagus, a rich salad sporting candied walnuts that Tyrell adored more than he wanted to admit, and all the wine they could drink. The wait staff was unobtrusive, helping to create a private moment for him and Vivienne. Then the waitress returned with dessert — a small chocolate dome covered in raspberry and chocolate ganache. Vivienne declared it divine, and Tyrell wanted to lick the plate.

After eating, they sat in the plush booth, finishing their robust red wine and trading burning looks and soft words. Tyrell placed his wineglass on the table and reached his long ebony fingers across to her dainty, manicured ones. He brushed his fingertip along the length of her hand, electricity sparking on her smooth skin. Vivienne's heart raced as she lifted her whiskey-colored eyes to his unbelievably deep black ones, like mysterious pools, and she lost herself in his intense gaze.

It had been a long time since she felt anything like this with a man. Her ex didn't seem to try too hard and never looked at her as though she was the only person in the room. Tyrell's eyes did look at her that way, as if his eyes could not leave her. And his gaze lit her insides on fire.

Tyrell felt that same electricity, that same fire, his heart thudding in his chest in wild movements. Friends may tease him that he was a player, but with Vivienne, all other women fell away. There was only her, and she was all he wanted, now and forever.

Eight

"Want to come back to my place?" he offered. Tyrell was bold, only one real date in, and he feared it might ruin his chances with Vivienne. But he couldn't stop himself. His whole body felt ready to burst if he didn't kiss her, hold her, lose himself in her.

Vivienne didn't answer. Instead, she leaned her amazing breasts across the table, giving him one of the best views he'd had in his lifetime, her face a scant inch from his. She placed her lips gently on his own.

The kiss was light, like a kiss from a specter, allowing that electricity to jump from her lips to his. She worked the kiss expertly, never pressing more than a faint hint. Her lips touched and retreated, then touched again, the tip of her tongue sliding along his lower lip.

Tyrell, who long considered himself a master of the romance game, had never been kissed so thoroughly in his life. His dick hardened to the point he was certain his cock would burst before they left the table.

She pulled back ever so slightly, keeping that brazen view of her full tits directly in front of his eyes.

"Yes," she breathed.

Tyrell kept his gaze riveted on her, getting drunk on those whiskey-shaded eyes, nearly forgetting the question he'd asked. He lifted his arm in the air.

"Bill, please," he announced to the passing server.

It took every ounce of willpower Tyrell possessed to drive the speed limit home. He wanted to race like he was a driver in the Indy 500, bust into his bedroom, and claim her hard and fast. But he needed to keep his cool, not behave like some unexperienced middle-schooler. His attempts to appear under control were feeble at best; his insides shook with a new and exhilarating excitement.

He parked the car like a madman, barely inside his shared carport. Remembering to keep his manners about him, Tyrell shimmied to her side of the car and opened her door — a true gentleman. He slammed the door shut and held out his arm to escort her inside, but she didn't grasp it. She placed her hand on his jaw, claiming his lips again instead.

This time, though, the kiss was far from a suggestion — it was deep and forceful, her tongue pressing into his mouth, teasing his tongue in an erotic dance. Keeping his arms wrapped around her waist, he urged her to his doorway, their lips continuing their erotic movements.

Tyrell's apartment, for the most part, was plain. Contractor white walls, a basic white kitchen, a gray couch in an undecorated living room. Not that Vivienne noticed his decor very much, her lips otherwise engaged with Tyrell's searching mouth as he banged through his own door.

One strong, large hand pressed against her lower back, and Tyrell let his fingers linger just above the curve of her ass where her muscle blossomed out curvy and full, begging for him to grab it. His other hand was where he had wanted it all night, entwined in that mass of thick, multicolored hair, clasping her face as close to his as he could manage.

As if in a strange dance, he moved with her, pressing her backwards towards his bedroom, never releasing her full lips. His mouth and tongue searched and searched, and Vivienne found it difficult to catch her breath. Her hands held his tight, springy curls in her palms and allowed her nails to scratch against the shaved hair on the back of his neck. Chills and shivers flowed from his neck to his spine, and his cock throbbed and ached against the tight denim of his jeans.

Unlike the rest of the apartment, his bedroom was something from a spread in a catalog. The dark brown, almost black wood added elegance and contrasted well with the red and white down comforter that she sunk into as he lay her on his bed. Vivienne was not one to be coy, having already loosened the straps of her dress and pulling it low enough to show off her navy-blue lace bra against the tanned swells of her enticing tits.

"Blue?" Tyrell had expected to see black lingerie under a little black dress. He slipped an elegantly long finger under the strap on her shoulder.

"Cop-blue," she told him, her voice husky. "I thought it appropriate." One side of her mouth tugged into a sexy half-smile.

"Very appropriate," he agreed.

Tyrell pulled the strap off her shoulder, following its path with a series of kisses from her shoulder to the top of her arm. Vivienne sucked in her breath at the tingling sensation of his lips on her skin. He electrified every nerve ending she had, and she shrugged at her dress, exposing her other bra strap.

He did the same with that side, only this time with his tongue, as he worked the dress to her waist. Her full breasts sprung free from the confines of her top with a jiggle, and he took the offer. Pressing his face between the full globes, she gasped as he flicked his lips and tongue along the lacy edge of her bra on one breast, then on the other. The musky scent of her perfume, like spiced oranges, filled his senses and made his head swim.

Her nipples hardened under her lace bra, the only thing separating Tyrell's mouth from her bare skin. More electrified waves flowed from her breasts through her whole body as he played with one nipple through the thin fabric. His tongue teased and retreated, over and over, and Vivienne quivered. Reaching her fingertips to the edge of the lace bra, her slender fingers tugged the lace away, granting him full access to her luscious tits, and he took advantage of what she offered, licking and sucking until his head spun.

Impatience drove his urgency, and Tyrell yanked the rest of her dress over her rounded hips and ass, another set of globes he wanted to stick his face between, and down her muscular, shapely legs. Her navy panties matched the navy bra, the only barrier to her enticing, shaved crevice he wanted to expose.

Tyrell sat back on the bed, admiring her from above. Against the red and white, she was shimmering bronze and blue, an all-American celebration on the bedding, and he wanted to continue to stare while tear the rest of her lingerie off at the same time.

She sat up suddenly, the full waves of her hair spilling over her arched back.

"Your turn," she said, pushing her hand against his strong, defined chest. She could feel the thrumming of his heart under the thin silver fabric of his shirt.

Tyrell stepped off the bed and let his personal Victoria Secret underwear model strip him naked. Her own admiring gaze as she peeled his shirt off his shoulders made every hair on his body stand on edge, and his cock tugged and pulled, begging to sink deeply into the woman in front of him.

Vivienne finished removing his shirt, allowing her pointed fingernails to trail across his biceps and back. The muscles in his back flexed, moving in ebony tendons and sinew, each muscle a defined line across his back that she could trace. Her fingernails skipped from one shifting muscle to the next, causing goose pimples and shivers to spring across his skin. Tall, dark, and muscular, Tyrell was a dream she wanted to take her time to enjoy.

When she followed the movement with her tongue, Tyrell thought he'd leap out of his own skin. Her tongue was like the flicker of a flame that burned where she touched, and he let her fire consume him. He couldn't take the tease any longer, and as she moved her tongue over his back, he unzipped his jeans, sliding them off his long, powerful legs.

Vivienne squatted in front of him, helping him slide the pants over his equally elegant feet, then slipped her hands up his legs as she stood. Through his clinging boxers, she cupped his smooth, heavy balls in one hand, and Tyrell shuddered at the feel of her fingers working his sensitive sack.

He moaned as his mouth found her lips, and his fingers found the clasp of her bra. He pulled back, one eyebrow upraised. She nodded, capturing his mouth again as he deftly unclasped her bra with one hand. His other one had managed to find the swells of her ass, clutching possessively as her breasts sprang free from the lace that had barely kept them under control.

Groaning deep in his throat, he moved his lips from her mouth, along her neck to her dusky pinkish-brown nipples, licking and tugging at one, then the other, then back to the first. He couldn't get enough.

Vivienne guided him back to the bed, pulling at his shoulders. "Come join me," she whispered in his ear as she teased his earlobe, first with her breath, then with her teeth. Her fingertips danced along the developed muscles of his chest, shaking at the strength he held back. She continued that path down the perfect definition of his six-pack abs to the waistband of his boxer-briefs. He was built like a god, and Vivienne couldn't get enough of him.

Tyrell reached between them and pulled off his boxers, letting his dick probe forward, thick and pulsing. A few shades lighter than the skin on his chest, his cock was full and twitching and searching for her. He reached to his bedside table and opened the drawer which held a pharmacy of condom options. Grabbing a silver one, he tore the package open with his teeth and rolled the condom on as quickly as his hand could work the fitted rubber over his dick.

He couldn't wait any longer but pulled the navy lace panties far enough to expose her wet opening, shades of pink and brown, with only a small tuft of black hair perched atop her slit that he needed to own. Drawing the panties off her leg, he reached down with one finger and pressed between those lower lips, feeling her dripping readiness. He flicked his finger lightly over her button of nerve endings, and she bit back a squeal.

"Ready?" he asked, the tip of his bulging cock positioned to enter her. She nodded. "Oh yes, babe," she answered and spread her thighs to welcome him.

He didn't wait a breath before surging forward, entering her damp, warm pussy, letting it suck at his cock, pulling him further in. She groaned and heaved her tits upward as he shivered at the velvet sensation of caressing and thrusting.

Starting slow, he drew the moment out, the heat and electricity of their movements spinning out into the universe. Vivienne wrapped her legs around his hips, pulling him deeper and a clenching began deep in his belly, his balls contracting, and his mind left him.

"Harder," she urged him, biting at his earlobe again. "Harder."

His huge cock touched every part inside her, hitting her g-spot as the base of his pelvis rubbed against her love button, and every nerve in her body lit on fire. She screamed out his name as pulsing waves of pleasure swept over her from her hair to her toes.

Unable to control himself, Tyrell responded, pounding hard and fast, every pore of his body burning and electric. The sounds of her panting and moaning pushed him over the edge, and the rush of cum exploded from his depth.

He groaned heavily, shuddering once, then again, and collapsed onto her chest, his face fitting perfectly between her lush breasts. They remained like that, entwined and panting, waiting for the moment that spun out to return.

"Have you lived in Orange County your whole life?" he asked her as his fingertips drew lazy circles on the skin of her breasts and rib cage.

They had finally crashed back to Earth, regained their senses, and were taking the time to enjoy the peaceful glow that surrounded them. The quiet of the room enveloped them and the rustling wind outside serenaded as they lay under his comforter, legs and arms still wrapped around each other.

Tendrils of her hair fell askance, tickling the hairs on his arm and chest, twisting in his fingers, spilling over her shoulder. It was as though her hair was entwining them all the more, stopping anything from separating their bodies.

"Yeah," she responded. "I was raised here, went to school here, even got my degree at Orange County College." Tyrell wanted to ask if that was where she met the crazy ex, but sagely kept his lips sealed. Cuddling post sex did not seem the time to discuss exes.

"How about you?" she probed. "You live here your whole life?"

"Yep, me too." He pressed his full lips against the smoothness of her forehead. "I thought of going into the military, but did college until I was 21, then hit the police academy. Got a job in Tustin, so I didn't have to relocate, which was nice."

"If you could go somewhere, work or travel somewhere else, would you want to?" Her curiosity was piqued.

"Yep," he was quick to answer. "I always wanted to travel. I think I would start south. Brazil, for certain. I want to see Rio Di Janeiro. Then maybe Europe. And Australia. That would be the bomb. You?"

"Definitely Australia," she agreed. "And I'd like to go to Egypt. My grandmother was born there, before she married an American. I'd love to see where she grew up. So different from here, you know?"

"I can't imagine. But the pyramids, the Nile, that would be a trip to remember. If you ever go, take me with you." He tried to sound casual regarding the offer, but he knew if she invited him, he would move the world to try and go with her.

Vivienne lifted her head off his chest where she had been resting, her raven eyebrows almost touching her hairline. "That's a joke, right?"

Tyrell lifted his shoulders off the bed to turn and face her. "Naw, I'm not kidding. I would love to travel, and I can't think of anyone else I would rather go with."

She stared into his earnest eyes for several heartbeats, then settled back onto his chest.

"Why, are you leaving today or something?" Tyrell joked.

"No, not today," she answered, cuddling him harder.

They lay together, chatting lightly, until the early hours of the morning.

Nine

The night sky was bright with a full moon and stars that seemed to glimmer more than they ever had before. While Tyrell hated to drive Vivienne back home, preferring her to sleep in his arms all night, he felt lighter, as though he could touch those very stars shining so far away.

They joked together in hushed tones on the short drive back to her bungalow apartment. Parking outside her house, he walked her to her door, again, a true gentleman. Vivienne giggled at his efforts.

"You don't have to walk me to my door," she told him, her voice full of sultry humor.

"What gentleman would I be if I didn't?" Tyrell shrugged at her. "And I have to make sure you get inside safe. Just doing my job, ma'am," he teased.

Plus, he was hoping for another one of those mind-numbing kisses. Even if they hadn't had crazy sex in his bed, that kiss would have made the evening a winner for him.

"I think I'm safe with you," she played coy, wrapping her arms around his neck as they reached her doorway.

"Only outside the bedroom, baby," he whispered in that husky voice that made her knees go weak.

She wasted no more time, but pressed her lips against his again, this time both light and deep, a dizzying back and forth on his lips. He felt like his tongue was chasing hers as she kissed him, and he couldn't keep up. Where the hell did she learn to kiss like that?

Just as suddenly as she kissed him, she pulled away, jangling her keys and opening her door.

"Call me later?" she asked. *Oh, hell yes*, was his immediate thought.

"Of course. I'll call you after work tomorrow." He made to step away but paused and shifted back to her. "And text you throughout the day."

The smile that caressed her face caused his chest to soar — bright and bold and full.

"You better," she replied as she shut the door.

Tyrell all but stumbled back to his car. Vivienne absolutely entranced him, like he was hopped up on a heady drug, and with any drug, he already wanted more. He didn't know what was so different about her, so compelling, but he liked it.

With his mind drifting off, thinking of the next time he could see Vivienne, he wasn't paying as much attention to the darkened parking lot as he should have. At first, he thought it was just a play of the shadows as his headlights swiveled through the bushes. He shifted the car into drive to pull away, but that shadow didn't sit well with him. Shaking his head to focus, he recalled his coffee date the other day with Vivienne and the gall of her ex to spy on them. What if they guy was playing peeping Tom now?

He grabbed his phone and selected one of the on-duty officer's number. Officer Saira Matkins was patrolling this area, at least if he remembered correctly. He waited to hit send, pulling back up to the building and shutting off his lights. Keeping the phone tight in his hand, Tyrell exited the car on quiet toes, moving silently, completely in command of his reflexes.

He saw nothing amiss at the front doorway, but that didn't mean everything was as it should be. One thing he had learned on patrol was the most innocent looking situations could be the most dangerous. After he stepped to the side of the bungalow to inspect the empty bushes, Tyrell returned to the neat front door and knocked.

Vivienne answered with surprise and confusion in her eyes. She had been brushing out her hair so it cascaded in waves down her back like a creek in a dense forest. Wrapped in a fluffy robe, she was obviously getting ready for bed.

"Hey, I don't want to frighten you," he began, and her eyes shot wide open.

"Well, that doesn't make me feel not frightened!" she answered. He waved his hand up in apology.

"I know. I know. But did you hear anything in the house when you got here?"

"Hear anything? Like, hear what?"

"I dunno. Just, anything? Did you see anything wrong in the house?"

Vivienne shook her head, disbelief crossing her features, nuanced with a flare of anger. She stepped to the side to let him enter the small foyer area, and the awareness of why Tyrell was asking came over her.

"My ex. Did you see him or something? I didn't see him this time."

"Naw, nothing like that. I thought I saw something or someone outside, shadowy like. But it was probably nothing."

"Do you want to look around?"

Vivienne moved further into her carpeted living room, and Tyrell followed, his eyes scanning the interior of her apartment with laser focus. He was no longer the Tyrell she had a date with. He was now Officer Blaser, working overtime on her stalking case. Watching the shift from man to cop would have been fascinating if it weren't for the reason why he was in cop mode.

"Naw, I think—" was all he could say before glass shattered from the bathroom at the end of the hall. Vivienne screamed at the sound. Tyrell's whole body tensed as his arm moved in front of Vivienne, pushing her behind him.

"Stay here," he ordered, and she didn't have to be told a second time.

With the carpet muting the sound of his footsteps, he skulked to the end of the hall where the bathroom door stood ajar, giving him a peek inside the blue and white bathroom. Cursing himself for not carrying his off-duty weapon, Tyrell curled his hands into fists and took on a fighting stance. Hopefully, the former baseball player was out of shape.

"We know you're there! This is Tustin PD! Come out with your hands up!"

Tyrell counted to three then shoved the white panel door open, where it brushed against broken glass and nothing else. Whoever broke the window was gone.

Racing back through the living room, Tyrell ran outside, hoping to catch the person responsible. He didn't see anyone in the parking lot, or the late model sedan Vivienne's ex drove. He had to make the decision to scramble after the ex or check on Vivienne, and valor won out. He returned to the living room where Vivienne stood, her hands clasped under her chin.

"Was it him? Was it my fucking ex?" Her voice was high-pitched and panicky.

Tyrell wrapped her in his long, muscular arms, and she melted into his strong chest. They took the moment to get their emotions under control before investigating the bathroom.

"We don't know for certain it was the ex," he tried to rationalize as they approached the bathroom, although he knew he was lying. It's always the crazy ex, that much he knew.

Vivienne kept her toes on the carpet as she leaned into the bathroom to flick on the light and assess the mess. The only things out of place was the broken window and the glass littering the floor. Tyrell stepped lightly around the broken glass to the window. His eyes searched the room for a rock or something that could have caused the damage, but nothing stood out. His eyes glanced across the broken shards still in the windowpane, looking for hairs or fibers, perhaps from a ripped shirt or jacket. There was no evidence that he could see with the naked eye. Time to call in the big guns.

"It could have been kids throwing rocks," Tyrell felt like he was lying again. "But just to be on the safe side, we should call the police. I have an officer's number already on my speed dial."

Vivienne pursed her lips at having to involve the police again, more than Tyrell that was, over what was most likely her ex acting like a fool. But she nodded anyway.

"And one more thing." He knew she wouldn't be happy with his recommendation. "Do you have a friend you can stay with tonight? Family? I want to get that window boarded up and until we can get it fixed, I just don't feel it's safe here."

Vivienne huffed at his suggestion. As much as she hated the idea of staying with someone else, Tyrell was right. He had probably seen situations like this before, more than she had anyway, and she should take his advice.

"Ok. You get on the phone to your cop, and I'll get on the phone to my parents. Let them know I'm coming over."

Tyrell immediately pulled out his phone and made the call. Vivienne picked her phone up off the narrow kitchen island and called her mom, who read the riot act over the phone, punctuating the conversation with statements of how she didn't like that guy in the first place.

"The officer should be here in a minute or so. She just finished a call and is only a few blocks over."

"Is this gonna be another police report?" she asked with a touch of irritation. Tyrell couldn't blame her. He grinned sheepishly.

"Yep. Officer Matkins will take that report."

"Oh, no more overtime for you?" she quipped, trying to make a joke after the crappy ending to their date night. Tyrell's mood improved with her humor.

"Yeah, I think I've worked enough overtime tonight as it is," he joked in return.

"My mom is pissed. She never liked Jason anyway. 'Preppy boy' she always called him. She believed he thought himself better than everyone else, you know?"

"Ahh," Tyrell tapped his chin in consideration. "So, if you dumped him, it was like saying you were too good for him, and his fragile ego couldn't handle it."

She pointed one of those green-tipped fingers right at him. "Bingo."

A shift in the lighting through the windows came only seconds before the heavy knock at the door. Tyrell opened it and welcomed Officer Matkins. He made brief introductions, then asked Vivienne to pack her stuff as he walked Saira to the busted-up bathroom. She did her check and noted her investigation as Tyrell checked on Vivienne.

She was throwing clothes into a pink and white duffel bag balanced on the edge of her creamy white bedding. Every move highlighted her frustration, and she was taking it out on her poor clothing.

"Ok, so, we will wait until Officer Matkins is done, and then she will want to take your report. We will head out to your parents then. I'll follow you there."

"Why will you follow me?" It seemed strange to her. After all, she was a grown woman who could drive herself.

"He already tried to run you off the road once." Tyrell didn't have to say who "he" was. His voice softened. "I would rather make sure you got there nice and safe."

The gesture touched her heart and made an imprint. She was afraid of falling for him too quickly, especially since he might get tired of this shit with her ex. But the way he treated her, everything he did and said — it seemed right. And she was falling for him, fast.

She dropped the shirt she was holding into the duffel and reached for him just as he reached for her. Their arms entwined. He leaned his head to hers, this time taking control of the kiss, hoping to let her know with his lips just how much she meant to him.

A sound of throat clearing caused them to jump apart, and the blush that spread across Vivienne's cheeks colored her face in a rosy hue he found endearing. Tyrell, on the other hand, gave Saira a shit-eating grin. She rolled her eyes at him.

"Hey, brother," she started, her tone announcing it was time to quick messing around and take a freaking report.

"Hey," he responded. "Did you find anything?"

"I'm gonna look outside before I go, but nothing but broken glass in the bathroom. He probably wrapped his hand in a jacket or something and punched it out. That's what it looks like to me. Can I get her statement now, or are you still busy?" She raised a mocking eyebrow, and this time Tyrell rolled his eyes.

"Yeah, yeah. I'll go start cleaning up the bathroom and cover that window." He directed his attention to Vivienne. "Broom? Cardboard?"

"Broom in the closet next to the kitchen. And I think there's an empty box in the spare bedroom that will work. Duct tape in the kitchen drawer next to the fridge." She pointed out her directions, and he gave her a comical salute as he left the room.

Once Officer Matkins completed the report, she stepped outside to check the perimeter of the bungalow. Tyrell had made himself useful, cleaning up the glass in the bathroom and covering the window with cardboard. They met Officer Matkins back in the living room.

"I don't see anything outside, but the bushes really make it difficult at night. I'll file the report, and we will keep a lookout for the ex. He has the warrant already, so we are looking hard." She waved to them as she left, heading out to the mean streets of Orange County.

Tyrell hefted Vivienne's pink and white bag into her car and followed her to her parent's house on the other side of town. Since it was late, and he didn't want to intrude more than they already had, he told Vivienne to say hello to her parents and that he looked forward to meeting them. And since they were right outside her parents' doorstep, he gave her a chaste peck on the cheek before leaving.

"Call me tomorrow. Let me know how you're doing," he told her before he left for his own calmer, but lonely, apartment.

Once at home, Tyrell considered his relationship status with Vivienne. Perhaps it was too early to call it a relationship. He didn't know what it was, really. Two dates, if he didn't count her visit to the station or their chat at the hospital, and one fantastic fuck fest, and here he was, thinking relationship.

And mix into that her messed-up ex. He worried that he could think he was falling hard for her because he had become so invested with her plight against her stalker. But the guy was doing nothing more than making it more complicated for Tyrell. Did he want to be with Vivienne because he really liked her? Or was it only the pressing need to protect her, because that was his job as a police officer?

He texted and called her the next day. Tyrell found himself thinking about her more than he should, at times when his mind should really be focused on something else — like work. His chest fluttered at any prospect of seeing her, and his face lit up every time she texted him.

His brothers in blue may joke about his sexual prowess with women, and he played it up for all it was worth. But he was tired of just dating. He saw the relationships the other guys had, the plans they made. They had a person to unload the misery of a bad call, a hard arrest, a disgusting crime. Tyrell didn't have that person — he sure as hell wouldn't unload that crap on a random woman he hooked up with from the gym.

With Vivienne, everything was different. She was engaged with him as a person. She didn't come onto him because she saw a hot guy at the gym. With Vivienne, he was more than just the hot cop; he was a man with interests and ambitions, and she saw that in him.

Even more than that, he wanted to share in her joys and interests. When she talked about her trip to Egypt, he saw himself going with her.

There was no question. He had fallen for her, and hard.

Another text dinged on his phone, and that sappy grin reappeared on his face. This time, he had to laugh to himself. From her texts, it seemed her mother was on fire over the possible stalker ex, and she wanted to storm down to the police station and demand better protection for her daughter. Only after Vivienne explained her dates with "the cop" did Vivienne's mother stop her interrogation.

Also, according to her texts, Vivienne had to describe Tyrell in full detail so her mother would know she was dating an attractive cop. "He doesn't have one of those mustaches, does he?" she had asked Vivienne. The laughing emoji she sent brought a smile to his mustache-less face. Her texts suggested that her mother was much happier with her daughter dating a police officer rather than a "loser wanna-be athlete," as Vivienne's mother referred to Jason.

After the gym, he showered, shaved that handsome face, his sparkling eyes and strong jaw shining under the bald bathroom lighting. He evaluated his lips. Tyrell always considered growing a mustache as he got older, but after Vivienne's comment from her mom, he needed to reconsider.

At the station, discussion of Vivienne's ex was a low point in briefing. Fortunately, Tyrell's sergeant and Saira Matkins kept his name out of the announcements while explaining that a local hit-and-run/stalker had grown more aggressive. Conversation buzzed as the sergeant listed Jason Kane's offenses, and the driver's license picture did the man no justice. Just as Vivienne said, average. Light brown hair, brown eyes, average height, weight, and too many known associates to list.

Saira had driven around the neighborhood the night before, checking out some of the addresses Vivienne provided, knocking on doors. If anyone were at home, according to her report to the sergeant, they played stupid as to Jason's whereabouts. And while Saira was certain that Jason was hiding out at one of those houses, she had nothing to support it, other than her sense that the guy was close by.

A photo of his car and his plate number also flashed on the screen with a BOLO order. After trying to kill Vivienne (and Tyrell, really) with his car, then stalking her and trying to break into her house, Jason the ex was at the top of Tyrell's most wanted list, even if he wasn't on any other. Only now, with a warrant issued for his arrest and the knowledge that Jason was staying close to home, or at least close to Vivienne's home, the police could plan for some exigencies. Added patrol was assigned around Vivienne's neighborhood and workplace, and they were coordinating with other local police to keep an eye out. Jason had become a full menace to the city of Tustin, and the police would not let that stand.

Ten

Vivienne spent the week with her parents, something she both loved and hated, and when Tyrell took her out for another date, she made him laugh as she imitated her mother.

That next date was not what Tyrell expected. She had asked if, on Saturday morning, instead of his game of B-ball, he would work out with her. He had raised one full, black eyebrow at the request. Never had a woman he dated wanted to work out with him. Or they said they did, but never followed up. Going to the gym with her seemed intimate, personal, and he loved the idea.

They met early on Saturday morning, gym bags in hand. Afraid she'd want to take a Zumba class with him, he offered up a morning of lifting, and her soft brown eyes lit up brightly. Relief flooded through him as he escorted her into the front doors.

Afterward, they went back to her house. Vivienne said it was because she needed another round of clothes.

"Unless you think I can stay here? My landlord fixed the window."

Tyrell settled his intense gaze on her beautifully worried face. Her pink lips pulled in as she weighed the joy of being home versus her own safety. Several loose hairs fell out of her headband and danced around her damp face, like stripes across her glowing skin. He lifted a finger and wiped the fringe from her cheek.

"I would prefer that you stay with the 'rents, just until we find this guy. He could break in here again. The window wasn't replaced with steel."

She sighed, dragging her duffel back into her bedroom like a punished child. Tyrell had to bite back a laugh. Vivienne was not a woman used to doing something she did not want to do. Yet, he was surprised she didn't fight him over it. Scanning his eyes around the room before following her, that notion stuck in his head. She should have fought him harder about coming back home. His brow wrinkled as a stark realization came over him.

"Vivienne!" he called down the hall, popping his head into her bedroom. "Are you afraid of this guy? Like really afraid?"

She didn't look at him as she packed, her arms moving in a steady pattern of folding. And she didn't answer.

"Vivienne?" his voice softened.

"Yeah, a bit. Like I dated that guy." She turned to face him, her eyes blazing. "I thought he was good enough to date and the whole time he was really this bad dude. I feel stupid, you know. And now he's stalking me and making things difficult for us—"

"Whoa," Tyrell snapped his head up. "What do you mean, difficult for us?"

"Um, hello Tyrell? Haven't you noticed that every time we've had a date, he's somehow interrupted it? It's like every date was tainted by him. And that's a lot for you to take on, even if you *are* a cop, to have a girlfriend with a crazy ex –"

"Are you my girlfriend?" he interrupted, his fiery onyx eyes softening.

"Well, I mean . . ." she stuttered, suddenly realizing what she just said. Her own heated gaze rose to meet his.

Tyrell didn't hesitate. He stepped forward, crushing her tense, tight body to his, kissing her mouth in a hard and messy meeting of lips and tongue. But he didn't stop there. He wanted to tell her how much she had come to mean to him, show her, and the only way he knew how to do that was with his hands and lips.

He knocked her colorful duffel from the bed and pressed her to the comforter, her bronzed skin a stark contrast to the creamy white and a compliment to his own skin. Tyrell loved the way his ebony skin looked when pressed to hers, all the colors of sand and earth among the clouds, meeting in passionate harmony.

They tore at each other's clothes — desperation and uncertainty in life made for heightened passion and desire, and the complications of her life lately fit the bill.

Tyrell pulled desperately at her neon sports bra and tight leggings, trying to get her clothes off her as quickly as possible. The heat inside him threatened to explode. She still had her shoes on, and he flung them across the room, tearing her leggings off her feet. Vivienne's movements mirrored his, tearing his clingy, sweaty tank top from his chest. He couldn't get close to her, touch her, come inside her, fast enough.

Their clothes littered the bed and the floor as Tyrell pushed her back down on the bed, planting his face between her legs. She squealed, protesting at how she'd smell after her workout, and he did nothing but inhale deeply, letting her know he didn't care. The smell of sweat, her own musk, and a spicy scent (*her shower gel? It's sexy as fuck,* he thought crazily) surrounded him as he buried his face between her intimate folds.

His own body thrummed and throbbed as he touched the tip of his tongue to her pink bud. Her body jolted off the bed, and he grinned at her reaction. Tyrell continued to play her like a violin until she was taut and shivering and panting.

Reaching for his wallet, he grabbed a condom out of its pocket and rolled it over his pulsating cock, the head nearly purple as it strained for Vivienne's dripping opening. His hands shook, and his body ached for her.

He rose above her, kissing her so she could taste her own juices on his lips, and entered her hard and fast at the same time. His cock pulsed as he did so, as though everything inside him wanted to leave him, explode from him, and fill her at once. Tyrell quivered as Vivienne dragged her nails over the thick muscles of his back to clasp at the perfect marble-strong globes of his ass.

Keeping her lips attached to his, she lifted her hips, rising and pushing as he worked against her. Vivienne's mind spun out of control as another orgasm pooled low in her abdomen and sizzled over every nerve, her body singing as his movements consumed her.

Her feminine lips dragged against his groin, pulling and stroking his thick cock in a mind-numbing rhythm. Every squeal that spilled from Vivienne's sweet mouth drove Tyrell closer to the brink. His own body began to shudder and tremble while Vivienne, rising higher as she clung to him, cried out his name over and over, and reached her height. His own thrusting overtook him, uncontrollably, and she bit at his lips. He called out to her, urgent and panting. And this time, everything inside him did erupt, and he was lost.

When he finally lifted his muscular body off Vivienne's own ample breasts, he lay on his back, his breathing heavy. *How did she consume him so much?* His eyes remained riveted on her heaving body, and he was awed. Every time he was with her, Vivienne filled his thoughts, his body, and he wanted more of her.

As his mind rolled these thoughts over, Vivienne reached across the short expanse of her bed that separated them and grasped his hand. Such a simple gesture, so innocent after the electrifying sex they just shared, but it was as though she held his heart in her palm, not his hand. Delicate, complete. Vivienne didn't want to stop touching him, and he was of the same mind. Tyrell squeezed her hand gently and received a slight squeeze back in return. He was smitten and hoped she felt the same way — or at least close.

"We need to do that more often," Vivienne's husky voice broke the silence. "I like ending my workout this way."

"Oh, that is something I can get behind." Tyrell tipped his head to give her a lazy smile.

"Mmmm, I'm sure you could," she agreed. "And a much better memory of being in my house than last time."

"Yeah," he agreed. "I would much rather get busy in bed with you than clean up broken glass."

Gathering up what energy he had left, Tyrell forced his lean form off the cushy bedding and started gathering his clothes. As he stepped into his gray mesh shorts, his eye caught some paperwork on Vivienne's dresser. Picking up a brochure, he turned to her, his eyes sparkling at her shapely body draped over her coverlet. She reminded him of a 1940s pin-up girl, and he felt that familiar stirring in his groin. Blinking to refocus, he held up the brochure.

"You weren't kidding."

Vivienne was busy staring at his chest and missed his comment.

"What?" she asked.

"Egypt?"

"Oh." She blushed a bit, and Tyrell liked how he could see it travel across her skin to her chest. That full, sexy bustline. "Well, I told you I wanted to do it."

"Yeah, but I was thinking of way in the future. That's usually what bucket lists are. At least to me. You're wantin' to go soon?"

The notion of her leaving him for a week or more on a vacation on the other side of the globe unnerved him, and he wasn't completely sure why.

Vivienne shook her head, her tortoise-shell hair shaking around her shoulders as she pulled it from the headband. She lifted herself off the bed and grabbed the brochure from his hand. Glancing through it, she tossed it on the bed next to her.

"I've got the money saved up, and I already talked to work about doing some of it remotely so I can get an extra week off. I'd like to do a two-week trip, Egypt and Morocco."

Tyrell's eyes widened. He picked his tank top off the floor and pulled it over his head before asking his next question. "When are you going, then?" He tried not to hold his breath.

"That, well, that's the problem." Vivienne scooted to the edge of the bed and began pulling on her own leggings. Tyrell sighed as she covered those sexy legs. "I don't know. I want to go soon. I've heard spring is amazing. But none of my friends can get the two weeks off. I don't want to go by myself —"

"I don't blame you," Tyrell interrupted. "Not just being in a foreign country alone. That would be scary enough for anyone, but it's more fun to go with someone else. I get that."

"Yeah," Vivienne agreed, shrugging into a t-shirt, leaving her sports bra on the bed. "So right now, the trip is on hold. I'll see what happens after Christmas. Maybe I can convince someone to go."

She deliberately kept her eyes averted from him. Going with the attractive man standing before her had crossed her mind more than once, but she didn't want him to feel any pressure from her. She had already slipped with the girlfriend comment.

Tyrell crossed his strong arms over his chest as he watched her finish dressing. "Maybe you aren't asking the right person."

She flicked her eyes to him, and he lifted one eyebrow in a suggestive question.

"What, you?" Surprise filled her. Taking a big, expensive trip was a large move in a relationship, and she was still hesitant if she should call him her boyfriend. Tyrell, though, seemed more secure in what they had going on. He had a strong self-presence, and it exuded from him like cologne.

"Why not? I haven't had the chance to travel a whole lot, and I have quite a bit of vacation time I can take."

"Are you serious?" Her brows furrowed as she stared at him.

"Why wouldn't I be?"

"Because, well, because —"

"Because it's only been like a month or so with us?"

"Yes! What if we book the trip, and then —"

Tyrell could not suppress the grin that popped onto his face. "What if I end up another crazy ex?"

"YES! That's so much pressure!" she exclaimed again. This time Tyrell laughed aloud.

"Then we have to make sure we are still together when we take the trip."

Vivienne paused before lifting her eyes to his. "Are you my boyfriend, then?" Her voice softened at the question.

"It's what I tell everyone. I call you my girlfriend. Isn't that what we are?"

She nodded, and he leaned over, enclosing her in his arms. Vivienne allowed herself to melt into him, into the security and positivity he put out into the world, put out for her. With Tyrell by her side, she felt like she could accomplish anything.

And little nuisances, like her ex, were nothing to worry about.

Eleven

Tyrell's chest heaved with hope and anticipation of solving the ex-boyfriend problem when he heard the news at briefing that night — two day-shift patrol officers found Jason's boring gray sedan parked at one of his associates' houses, one of the same guys who said they hadn't seen Jason in weeks. *Fuckin' liars,* Tyrell thought to himself as the sergeant droned on.

The sedan was now in impound, so the ex was without a car, but that didn't mean he didn't have another car, or the "friend" wouldn't lend him one. Tyrell scratched at the tight curls on the back of his neck, considering the whole situation. Really, they weren't any better off with the impounded car. The ex surely wasn't stupid enough to try to get the car out of impound. He would know why it was there.

But Tyrell had to remain hands-off for most of the investigation and policing that involved Vivienne's ex. His recent relationship with her would not only complicate the investigation, the department would certainly view it as a conflict of interest at the least, a firing offense at worst. And if it went to court? His relationship with the vic would surely complicate the D.A.'s case.

Matthew's navy-clad form marched down the hall. He paused when he reached Tyrell, his stance wide and his hands resting on his belt. His beat partner, Matthew Danes, was a true brother in blue and gave him the details on what the cops had uncovered. Unfortunately, it was not much.

"No updates yet, brother." Disappointment tinged Matthew's voice. "The guy's sedan is beat to shit though, crushed, with trails of dark red paint transfer along the right side. There's no doubt his car is the one that hit your black and white and then hit hers."

"So, we got the warrant out for the hit and run, and for the stalking, too?" Tyrell wanted to make sure they were missing nothing.

"Yeah. The D.A. wants to add attempted murder and even assaulting a police officer. And vandalism for the broken window. Until we know more, we're blaming him. We are also dotting all the I's and crossing all the T's to make sure he doesn't walk on some technicality."

Tyrell nodded, looking past Officer Danes toward the open door leading to the parked patrol cars. *That can NOT happen,* he thought.

"Has it gotten serious with Vivienne?" Matthew raised one blonde eyebrow in interest, changing the subject.

Tyrell rubbed a manicured hand over his smooth chin, trying to hide the smile that tugged at his cheeks. Matthew shot a grin back.

"What happened to Blaser the player? Did he retire?"

Rocking his head in contemplation, Tyrell's smile widened. "Yeah, if he was ever there, he retired. I want something more, you know?"

Oh, Blaser. It's like that? Way to go." He clapped Tyrell on the back, and Tyrell's smile nearly split his face. He cackled, then collected himself.

"Yeah, brother. It's like that," he admitted.

Tyrell found himself doing something he never believed he would: preparing for his two-month anniversary with Vivienne since their inauspicious meeting on the side of Newport Road.

The last few weeks had been quiet. Vivienne's ex seemed to fall off the planet, and police interest in finding him waned as time passed. While the warrant for his arrest was still out, they had no leads. He hadn't shown up at one of his jobs, so his company fired him. But he still had his under-the-table work. His college ball buddies said they had not seen him, but the cops knew they were lying. They were hiding him well. While Jason may have run away to his parents up north, he would've had to take a bus to get there. Jason Kane didn't seem like a bus-taking guy.

Vivienne, much like the police, was ecstatic over Jason's absence. Her dates with Tyrell didn't end with him chasing her ex and her making bad "working overtime" jokes whenever they went out. Her focus was on her man, her handsome cop, where it should be. They talked about the upcoming holidays like a normal couple. And the fact she was finally able to move back into her apartment was also welcome. Vivienne loved her bungalow apartment, easily breakable windows notwithstanding. And Tyrell loved being in that bungalow with her.

Her friends and coworkers got more than their fair share of cop-boyfriend tales now that Vivienne's mind wasn't on her own safety. Vivienne's closest friend and coworker, Janelle, was over the clouds at Vivienne's relationship with Tyrell. She had believed Jason was a loser to begin with.

To compare him to Tyrell was to compare an ass to a stallion, Janelle told Vivienne one day after Tyrell, in full uniform, stopped by the insurance office. Taller than average and filling out the full uniform with chiseled muscles and a flirty smile, he garnered appreciative glances from both the women and the men in the office.

While her schedule was flexible, and she often worked at home, Mondays always found her in the office.

"I just got off work," he told her, as it was early morning.

He stood erect next to her desk, resting his hands casually on his gun belt, *full cop-stance,* she thought. Having him stand before her in uniform sent a mix of danger and excitement surging through her veins. She stretched her neck to look up at him.

Even after a full night on duty, chasing criminals and dealing with less-than-desirable people, he looked unbelievably fresh, alert, and enticing. Vivienne wanted to rip the uniform off him right there. She'd send him a text later, telling him to wear the uniform the next time they were alone.

She stood up and kissed him chastely. Tyrell thanked God that it wasn't one of her nibbling kisses that drove him crazy. He wanted to sink his hands into her marbled hair as it was.

"What are you doing here?" she asked, her amber eyes wide with surprise. "Do you need some insurance for your car or something?"

Tyrell chuckled, shaking his head. "Naw, nothing like that. But when I do need insurance, you are the first person I'm seeing."

Janelle tipped back in her chair, her slick black hair dangling almost to the floor as she peeked past her cubicle to appraise Tyrell. His back was to her, and she gave Vivienne a thumbs up. Vivienne waved her off with a quick twitch of her hand and directed her attention to Tyrell.

"It's just, you got to see where I work," he continued, seeming oblivious to the attention he was receiving from the office staff, "so I thought I'd come by yours to say hi."

"Well, I would give you a tour, but," she swept her hand around the room separated only by short cubicle walls, "this is it." She grinned at him. "Did you bring me cookies?"

Tyrell's chest, thick with the added girth of his bullet-proof vest, shook as he laughed. "I don't think you'd want to eat any cookies I made," he admitted. "And you already have my number. I just wanted to see you before I went home today. I didn't want to wait until later this week."

Vivienne's heart fluttered, and a rosy blush colored her cheeks. Pulling Tyrell's smooth jaw into her soft hands, she pressed her lips to his once more. She jerked back quickly, hoping no one noticed her interlude. Only Janelle was still peeping, giving Vivienne another thumbs up. Vivienne rolled her eyes.

"Aw, babe," Vivienne gushed, full of fluttery emotion. "I am so glad. I didn't want to wait to see you either."

"Well, I don't want to keep you." Tyrell started to step away. "We still on for a workout tomorrow? After you get off work?"

Vivienne nodded, her shimmery hair falling about her elated face. Tyrell kissed the top of her head before he left, not wanting to make more of a scene than he probably had already. Janelle and a few other workers leaned their chairs to the edges of their cubicles to watch his tight, uniformed rear end walk out the door.

"Oh, he's a hottie! I'm sure you will 'get off' tomorrow!" Janelle laughed to Vivienne after making her asses to horses comment. Her running commentary only made Vivienne blush all the more. Janelle practically hooted at her reaction.

"You really like him, Viv!" she exclaimed.

Vivienne didn't deny it. "I hate to say he's a nice guy, but he is! And he just takes care of stuff. Super thoughtful with me, like coming in to say hi today. He does stuff like that!" Her voice shared her shock that a man could be as considerate as Tyrell.

"Well, good," Janelle's tone was authoritative. She had no problems telling Vivienne what she thought of her friend's social life. "You deserve a good guy. And for your hot cop to stop by after pulling a long shift just to say hi? I think he likes you a lot, too."

Vivienne's chest fluttered at the prospect. She could only hope so, since she had fallen in love with her handsome cop.

Twelve

They decided on an easy movie night on Tyrell's couch, complete with a bowl of popcorn and the latest horror flick. They cuddled under the blanket as California's winter rain poured down outside, and the night was so cool it could almost be called cold. Vivienne felt more comfortable over the past couple of weeks, having moved back into her own home, and the night felt cozy.

They both sported cushy sweatshirts after their workout, and Tyrell laughed at the extra-fluffy socks she pulled on after she arrived. They snuggled under a fluffy blanket to fend off the damp weather. Throughout the movie, Vivienne screamed and hid her eyes at the scary parts while Tyrell teased her over her reactions.

"Why do you like to watch these movies if they scare you so much?" he asked.

"They don't scare me like that," she told him. "It's more the jump scare thing—" she started to explain when a crashing sound came from Tyrell's bedroom.

"What the hell?" Tyrell rose from the couch in one fluid movement. His entire visage changed; his body tensed. He held up a hand at Vivienne. "Stay here, babe."

Vivienne sat tall on the couch, listening for Tyrell. As soon as he stepped from the room, the pizza delivery person knocked at the door.

"Pizza's here!" Vivienne called out and rushed to the door to pay for the pizza so the guy could get out of the rain.

Just as she turned the knob, Tyrell yelled from the hallway. "Don't open the door!"

Vivienne turned her head to see what he was yelling about when the door burst open, flinging Vivienne to the side.

Jason stepped into the apartment like he owned it, dripping on the carpet, waving a long carving knife in Vivienne's face. He kicked the door shut as he advanced on Vivienne.

"Who the fuck lives here, Viv?" he yelled, his face red with anger or exertion, she didn't know. His eyes popped from his head, a crazed look she hadn't seen before. She stepped away and the wall bumped against her back. There was nowhere left to go.

"Why are you here, Jay?" She tried to wrap her brain around the fact that her ex was standing in her current boyfriend's living room. All she could hear in her head was an echo of *What the hell?*

Jason jerked as if to move closer to her, pressing the knife to her face, when he was body slammed into the closed door. His arm with the knife was forced up as it hit the door, knocking the knife from his hand. It fell to the floor at their feet.

At seeing a strange man in his home, Tyrell shifted from the relaxed boyfriend to the engaged cop. Two thoughts careened through his mind as he raced toward the invader: *Disarm the perp; control the situation.* He became another person, even as he lacked the requisite uniform.

Tyrell's entire body held the invader immobile against the door as he kicked the knife away. Every muscled tensed and flexed as he kept Jason under control. Vivienne remained frozen in her place, shocked at the fight, such as it was, and watched with panicked eyes.

"Call 911, Viv," Tyrell told her in a tone she had not heard since she first met him when he pulled her over for the traffic stop. *His cop voice,* she thought crazily, strangely calm and commanding.

It took her a moment to move. Jason was trying to fight back and wriggling to get one arm free. "I'm gonna get you, Viv!" he yelled as he struggled.

Tyrell wrestled with him as Jason fought back, then worked him around, pressing Jason's face against the wall next to the door and holding Jason's hands behind his back. Tyrell kept one shoulder firmly lodged against Jason to hold him in place. There was no way he would allow this psycho to hurt someone he loved.

"Stop fighting, man," Tyrell commanded in that same, authoritative voice. "I'm a cop, the police are on their way." He flicked his head to Vivienne to get her to grab the phone. "And I don't want to have to choke you out. I will, don't get me wrong. But don't make me do it. It won't be pleasant for you."

Jason continued to struggle and yelling "Viv!" and some other random nonsense she ignored as the 911 dispatch answered. Vivienne rattled off their current situation and Tyrell's address.

"Give them my badge number, babe," he told her as she spoke into the phone. "4546."

Vivienne repeated the number to the dispatcher who promised help was on the way. She clicked off the phone and lifted her dazed eyes to Tyrell. He wrestled Jason to the ground but threw a look over his shoulder at Vivienne as he did so.

"Babe, can you go into the bedroom? Top left drawer of the dresser has a set of handcuffs. Get them?"

His stern poker faced never shifted, nor did his attention to the guy he had on the floor. Vivienne nodded once then raced into the bedroom.

She returned and handed the cuffs to Tyrell, who took them with an expert grasp. His arms tight and flexed, he held Jason still as he snapped the cuff on his left wrist and wrenched Jason's hand against his back.

"Gimme your other hand," Tyrell growled, leaning over Jason's prone body. Resigned, Jason lifted his right hand off the floor, and Tyrell grabbed it, snapping it in the other cuff.

Only then did Tyrell sit back on his heels and exhale.

After Tyrell got Jason handcuffed, he left the guy laying on his floor and reached for Vivienne. The look on her face reminded him of the first night he met her, after her Jeep was side-swiped by the same asshole presently resting on his carpet: full of shock and disbelief. Tyrell had to restrain himself from giving the ex a swift kick in the head for causing her so much trauma.

"You Ok, babe?" Tyrell asked, pulling her as close to him as possible, as if his arms could protect her from all the miserable in the world. He couldn't — that he knew. Even as a cop, his protective reach was limited, but here in his house, with him, he'd keep her safe.

"Yeah, yeah. I think." Vivienne sounded calm, not quite the shocked voice he recalled from the traffic stop.

She twisted her head around to glance at Jason who had quieted and almost appeared asleep. He realized he was defeated.

"What happens with him now?" she asked.

"Well, he'll go to jail tonight," he answered with certainty. "He's got a warrant for the hit and run and the stalking, so he'll stay in jail most likely. If he does get out on bail —" Tyrell looked at Vivienne with stern eyes, "and I mean *if*, then the DA will take it to trial quickly. But if he gets a good lawyer, I'm sure he will cut a deal for immediate, but reduced, prison time."

"Good. Let's hope he doesn't get out on bail. I'm so done with him."

Vivienne glared at the man on the floor. If looks could throw daggers, Jason would have had a lot more to worry about. Sirens sounded in the distance as blue and red tinted the windows in a subtle hue. The cavalry had arrived.

Tyrell kissed her forehead and helped her off the floor, ready to answer the door.

"Brother, you shouldn't work your own cases at home!" Officer Jaden Sinacore laughed at Tyrell as he entered the house. Tyrell shook his head. Jaden always found the joke in any situation. Just as quickly as he joked, Officer Sinacore's hazel eyes turned fierce, focusing on the perp on the floor.

"The sarge is on his way. He's gonna wanna take your statement," he told Tyrell, then flicked his eyes to Vivienne. "But if you are cool with it, I'd like to take her to the kitchen and get her statement. Jonesy is on OT tonight, so he'll play clean-up to your friend here."

"He is *so* not my friend," Vivienne piped up as she listened in on their conversation.

Jaden nodded politely, then returned his focus to Tyrell. "You good, brother? Taking down a wanted man in your own apartment all by yourself. I know you want to look like the hero to the girl but come on!" Jaden's joke pulled a slight smile from Tyrell's rigid face.

The radio on Jaden's shoulder squawked. He tipped his head toward the noise, his spiky brown hair dancing in the red and blue strobe light in the apartment, which only grew brighter as other cops arrived.

By the time Officer Sinacore took her statement, the apartment was packed with navy blue uniforms, clipboards, and chatter as the police removed Jason to the back of Jonesy's black and white and finished their investigation. To Vivienne, it looked like a cop movie was being filmed in the apartment.

Vivienne and Tyrell gave their statements, and then, almost as sudden as Jason's violent entry, everyone departed. Officer Sinacore was the last to go, leaving Vivienne with instructions on what would happen next and clapping Tyrell on the back, asking once more if he didn't need to go to the hospital. Tyrell shook his head and all but shoved the laughing Jaden out the front door.

Once everyone left, and the night fell back into quietude, Tyrell locked the door and shifted his gaze around the living room. Vivienne followed suit, then stepped toward the couch to push it back into place.

They spent the next few minutes cleaning up from the invasion, contemplating everything that had transpired that evening. It was not the date night they had planned.

"You sure you're okay?" Tyrell asked. "Like, with everything? If this goes to court or whatever?"

Vivienne cast her shimmery gaze around the room that again resembled Tyrell's living room. Her marbled hair was disheveled, and strands that had pulled free from her messy bun kept getting caught on her eyelashes. Her hand absently wiped at her face, trying to keep her hair out of her eyes.

"Yeah," she finally spoke. "It's done. So, everything else, it's, well, like closure. I get to close the door on that guy, finally."

She lifted her eyes to Tyrell's soft, inviting gaze. "And step through a different, open door," she ventured. "Only with less overtime."

Tyrell's chest leapt at the prospect of walking through that door of opportunity with this amazing woman. His lips pressed gently against hers.

"Best overtime I ever worked."

The End

If you loved this book, please leave a review and check out the next book in the series, Holiday Pay!

Bonus Police Ebook

Don't forget to grab your **bonus ebook** police romance ebook starter! Click the image below to receive *On Patrol*, a pulled-from-real-life short story in your inbox, plus more freebies, ebooks, and goodies!

Then, check out my other *Tactical Protectors* series, my police series, and ride along with the boys in blue! Look for *Night Shift* from the *Tactical Protectors* series today!

Click here: https://swordandthistle.myflodesk.com/bee17851-69cc-4148-a553-c97b2134f60b

Police Blotter

I would again like to extend a heartfelt thank you to all of my readers for taking a chance and reading this series. Here we are on book 3, and book 4 is on deck! Crazy!

As mentioned before, many of the police interactions you read in this series are pulled from actual events – modified and changed a bit for the story and to protect the identity of those involved. I also try to keep in mind that all different people, with different experiences and backgrounds, live in California and work as police officers. I hope reflecting that is done well and keeps the stories relevant to you who read them. Pulling from real life adds to the stories -- I want to keep it as real as possible for you, my amazing readers!

And as always, I would also like to thank my family for supporting me. They always assumed writing was my "real" job. For my encouraging children, Mommy has always been an author. And to my own mom, who saw her daughter get a degree in English, of all things, and made no judgments and instead remained confident that her daughter would be successful even with such an inauspicious field of study.

Finally, I would like to thank Michael, my own man in uniform, the man in my life who has been so supportive of my career shift to focus more on writing, and who makes a great sounding board for ideas. As my hero in blue, I appreciate the uniform and listen for the sound of his safe return home every night.

If you liked this book, please leave a review. Reviews can be bread and butter for an author, and I appreciate your comments and feedback!

Excerpt from Charming:

Mariah slapped her phone before it emitted another trilling beep. She had lowered the volume as far as she dared to still be able to wake up for class, but in the dark of night, the ringer still sounded far too loud.

The snoring body next to her grunted and Mariah froze. The apartment was quiet — she even held her breath to make sure she didn't make as sound either. Once the body settled, Mariah lifted the covers and slipped out, as stealthy as a thief.

And wasn't that what she was doing? Thieving her time away from Derek? Mariah tiptoed to the narrow walk-in closet, and only when the door was secure did she turn on the light.

She blinked in the sudden illumination and released the breath she held as she pulled down the loose tank top, hunter green duster sweater, and dress slacks she had selected the night before. Mariah hated eight a.m. classes and laid out her outfit the night before to cut back on the time it took to get ready.

Once dressed, she shut off the light and slipped to the kitchen to make a small pot of tea, then closed herself in the bathroom to apply a quick layer of makeup.

For a college professor in her late 20s, makeup should have been an area of expertise for Mariah, but having spent much of her late teens and early adult hood with her nose in a book, makeup had remained a mystery to her.

She was fortunate, however, that her lightly tanned skin only needed a quick application of BB cream and makeup that came in iridescent plastic kits, so all she had to do was open one kit and everything else was ready — eyeliner, shadow, mascara, a hint of blush and lip gloss. Her dark brown eyes were easily smoky, so that saved time as well.

Then came the bane of her existence — a fluffy mound of ash-blonde hair that was half wavy, half curly, and always a frizzy mess. Mariah called it her triangle mess. She pulled it into a bun or a banana clip nearly every day and called it good. Her hair was a disaster. She decided on a clip to keep it under control. It was too early to deal with her hair-disaster.

Zipping up her books, she grabbed a to-go cup of tea and her purse waiting by the front door, then peeked in her purse.

Her keys weren't in her purse.

Where the hell are my keys?

She pressed her head against the apartment door and exhaled.

In the bedroom. She had retrieved a book from her car last night before bed and left the keys on her bedside table.

Fuck.

Mariah pulled off her boots and, leaving them by the front door, slipped back into the bedroom which was still dark thanks to the room darkening curtains. She palmed the keys so they wouldn't jingle and made it to the bedroom doorway.

But she missed her count and banged the side of her head against the door jamb.

She held her breath again, sure that the banging woke Derek, but he continued to snore. His late night was paying off in her favor. Rubbing the side of her head, she made it back to the front door, zipped her boots back on, and left.

Escaped was more like it.

Once she was in her car, she fully breathed again.

"I can't live like this," she told herself.

She was an adjunct professor, making enough money to support herself, a feminist who was supposed to be a role model for her young college students, yet she lived with a narcissistic emotional abuser who gaslighted her on a regular basis.

Mariah was not proud.

Glancing at the clock in her car, she took a sip of her cooling tea and pulled out to the street toward campus.

Mariah's mind drifted as she drove the short trip. Not for the first time, she asked herself what she was doing with Derek. The past few weeks had become a living hell with the man, and she was still letting him sleep over and dictate how to live in her own home.

What the hell is wrong with me?

Why was she letting him do this? She wasn't that type of person. She didn't see herself as that type of person.

In fact, she'd been called a bitch to her face more than once. And she reveled in the term. Why not own it?

What had happened over the past years that made her think she deserved someone like Derek? That was the lone conclusion she could draw — that subconsciously she believed she wasn't deserving of someone better.

Who the hell am I?

But what if her subconscious was telling her something? What if she was only worthy of someone like Derek?

They had met at a bar, of all places.

By God, shouldn't that have been a clue?

Nothing but a meat market, and two of her friends outside campus dragged Mariah there on a Karaoke night. A tallish blond with a decent physique, at least what she could discern from the button down he wore — took the stage and belted out a decent rendition of *Don't Stop Believing*. Mariah had loved it and ended up cheering louder than anyone else in the bar.

The three shots of Fireball hadn't hurt either.

She got his number, made out with him in the parking lot, and called him later in the week.

Most of their dates had been to bars. That should have been her first clue.

But he was so sexy — with light eyes that squinted in a come-hither way that reached into her chest and squeezed her heart.

When was the last time she'd felt that with him? Mariah couldn't recall.

And he had a great job, so he wasn't leeching off her.

Slowly he'd started making requests of her, about her apartment or how she lived. And as much as she hated herself for it, she'd begun to walk on eggshells around him.

And they didn't do anything together. They didn't watch movies and eat popcorn on the couch. They didn't go to any campus events, even though the music festivals were fun. They didn't have long conversations late into the night. They'd eaten out together all of two times. No dates to the park, nothing. Was she overly romantic, or misguided to think that relationships should be more? All they shared was the bar and the bed.

The bar and bed.

He'd been decent enough in bed to start. Giving it his all the first time or two.

Mariah tapped her fingers on her steering wheel as she waited at a light. She also couldn't recall the last time she came when he was pumping into her. Lately, she'd begun to push him away, using the old "I have a headache" line.

Yeah. Something needed to be done.

She was done.

Check out the Campus Heat Series and Charming!

About the Author

M.D. Dalrymple is a pen name of Michelle Deerwester-Dalrymple, a professor of writing and an author. She has written articles and essays on a variety of topics, including several texts on writing for middle and high school students. She is presently working on a novel inspired by actual events. She lives in California with her family of seven.

Follow the author here: https://linktr.ee/mddalrympleauthor

Also By Michelle

<u>As Michelle Deerwester-Dalrymple</u>
<u>Swept into the Highland Past:</u>

Highlander's Dawn
Highlander's Awakening
Highlander's Morning

<u>Glen Highland Romance</u>

The Courtship of the Glen –Prequel Short Novella

To Dance in the Glen – Book 1

The Lady of the Glen – Book 2

The Exile of the Glen – Book 3

The Jewel of the Glen – Book 4

The Seduction of the Glen – Book 5

The Warrior of the Glen – Book 6

An Echo in the Glen – Book 7

The Blackguard of the Glen – Book 8

The Christmas in the Glen — Book 9

<u>The Celtic Highland Maidens</u>

The Maiden of the Storm

The Maiden of the Grove

The Maiden of the Celts

The Roman of the North

The Maiden of the Stones

Maiden of the Wood
The Maiden of the Loch - coming soon

<u>The *Before* Series</u>

Before the Glass Slipper

Before the Magic Mirror

Before the Cursed Beast

Before the Mermaid's Tale
Before the Emerald Crown

OVERTIME

Before the Red Cloak

Glen Coe Highlanders

Highland Burn – Book 1

Highland Breath– Book 2
Highland Beauty — Book 3

Historical Fevered Series – short and steamy romance

The Highlander's Scarred Heart
Her Highlander's Scarred Soul

The Highlander's Legacy

The Highlander's Return

Her Knight's Second Chance

The Highlander's Vow

Her Knight's Christmas Gift

Her Outlaw Highlander

Outlaw Highlander Found

Outlaw Highlander Home

As M.D. Dalrymple - Tactical Protectors

Night Shift – Book 1

Day Shift – Book 2

Overtime – Book 3

Holiday Pay – Book 4

School Resource Officer – book 5

Undercover – book 6

Holdover – book 7

<u>Campus Heat</u>

Charming – Book 1

Tempting – Book 2

Infatuated -- Book 3

Craving – Book 4

Alluring – Book 5

<u>*Tactical Protectors: Marines*</u>

Her Desirable Defender – Book 1

Her Irresistible Guardian — Book 2

Her Tempting Protector

Made in the USA
Middletown, DE
03 September 2024